MW00423058

THE GAMES MEN PLAY
CHECKMATE

BY

MARK D. CRUTCHER

Literally Speaking Publishing House

Washington, DC

www.LiterallySpeaking.com

2020 Pennsylvania Avenue, NW, #406

Washington, DC 20006

Visit our website at

www.LiterallySpeaking.com

Copyright © 2005 by Mark Crutcher

ISBN: 1-929642-50-4

Published by Literally Speaking Publishing House

LSPH hard cover printing 2005, Printed in the U.S.A.,
First Printing 10 9 8 7 6 5 4 3 2 1

L iterally Speaking Publishing House, one of America's fastest growing publishers of adult fiction and nonfiction hardcover as well as trade paperback books, is the publisher of several national bestsellers including *Blessed Assurance, Chocolate Thoughts, Mocha Love* and *Plum Crazzzy.*

With its upcoming titles, *Checkmate*: *The Games Men Play, Illusions, Nowhere To Turn, Don't Mess With Me, Journey to the Light, Forbidden Fruit, Preachers' Row* and *Speak to My Heart*, LSPH is dramatically expanding its diverse mixture of first-time and veteran authors who uniquely capture life's joys and pains, fears and hopes, pitfalls and successes through refreshing characters, creative story lines, and inspirational writing.

With its bold, refreshingly original and inspirational books, LSPH is becoming known throughout the nation as the home of "Writing that Speaks To You"—Writing that speaks to your experiences, dreams, desires, mind and most importantly, your heart. Welcome to the LSPH experience.

www.LiterallySpeaking.com

DEDICATION

First giving praises and glory to God. This book is dedicated to all women. I honor and respect you for the temperament it takes to be the women that you are.

ACKNOWLEDGEMENT

There are so many people who played a part in making this book a reality. I have truly been blessed to know all of you. I am afraid that if I try to list you all, I'd leave someone out. However, there is an elite group that commands mentioning.

To my parents, Emmer and Chubbie Crutcher, I love you both very much. I know you might have felt over the recent years that I abandoned the biblical teaching the two of you have instilled in me. But I have never forgotten about my heavenly Father from whom all my blessings flow.

To my siblings, Jeanette, Mitchell, Deloris, and Timothy, whom I have had the luxury of watching and learning from as I grew up. I have taken a little from each of you that has helped to make me into the man that I am today.

To my son, Mark Crutcher, I pray that I have been the father you want and need me to be. There have been times when you may not have understood my reasoning. But, I do everything for the betterment of you. I hope you are as proud of me as I am of you.

To my daughter, Cierra Crutcher, I know you often question my love for you. But know that I do love you very much. There are times that I find it difficult to communicate with you about the things that you are going through. But as you enter into your teenage years, I pray for the wisdom to help me understand and to be able to articulate the right words of encouragement that you will need at those pivotal moments in your life.

To my close friend, Jerome Rodgers. Without you I don't know how I would have made it through that heartbreaking experience after my break-up with the love of my life. Thank you for those countless days you provided an ear to listen and a shoulder to lean on.

To Bishop T.D. Jakes, I have learned so much from you over the past eight years under your tutelage. The "Seven Steps To A Turn-Around" sermon you preached has catapulted me into the purpose God would have for my life. May God continue to dwell richly in your life.

To my Memphis, TN connection, I just want to give a big shout out to everybody off of Summer Avenue and especially to Terry, Kevin, Larry, Walter, Scooter, Brain, Boo, DJ, Perry, Raymond, Sam, Pineto, Big Ford, John, and Dion.

To the entire Literally Speaking Publishing House Family, thank you for all of the support. Special thanks to Shaun Stevenson, Maurice Calhoun, Rod Dennis, S. James Guitard, and Paul Morgan. Extra special thanks to the team of editors led by Associate Editor J.M. Branch, Senior Editor Marie Carter and Executive Editor Mychelle Morgan.

TABLE OF CONTENTS

THE GAMES MEN PLAY
CHECKMATE

BY

MARK D. CRUTCHER

INTRODUCTION

For the first time in my life, I understand the pain that I have heard many women express. Pain they have endured after encounters with men who have pretended to love them. I can identify with the confusion they faced in not knowing what they had done wrong, because I, myself, cried until there were no tears left to shed. I, too, have suffered days that have turned into weeks of sleepless nights.

It all seems strange now. After all, I used to be the kind of man who caused such pain. You know the type—a ladies' man, a player, a pimp, the man with all the right words and all the right moves. I am not proud of my past or the way I treated women. I apologize to any woman that I hurt. And as I accept full responsibility for my actions, I believe I must take this one step further. It is time for me to stop taking and give back. As a matter of fact, it's time for men in general to do more than just take. The time has come for men to give up their "player cards" and the tricks that go with the trade.

In order to explain how I arrived at this decision, I must share some details of my past. For about 14 years, I was engaged in a game not unlike the game of chess. In a chess match, the objective is to place the opponent's king in an inescapable position on the game board. In the game I played, my objective was to persuade women to maintain casual, uncommitted, sexual relationships with me. By the time they realized that my intentions were purely physical, it was too late. They were already addicted to the experiences we had shared and could not or would not let go. Checkmate.

> "IN THE GAME I PLAYED, MY OBJECTIVE WAS TO PERSUADE WOMEN TO MAINTAIN CASUAL, UNCOMMITTED, SEXUAL RELATIONSHIPS WITH ME."

However, it was on a sad day a couple of years ago that I realized the tables could turn…and had indeed turned. You see, the woman I loved walked out of my life without any warning…ON OUR WEDDING DAY! This time I was left to pick up the pieces without any understanding or explanation of what had gone wrong. Before that day, I was sure we would be in love for the rest of our lives. Yet, on a beautiful fall afternoon, I stood proudly wearing a white tuxedo in the presence of family and friends, waiting for my bride to walk down the aisle. As the music played, everyone smiled and waited anxiously. But she never showed. There I stood, brokenhearted, lost, confused, and alone.

Words cannot express how I felt. I thought to myself, "How could this happen to me? I am a master of the craft. I am at my peak. I am the man." What I didn't realize was that this time I was playing the game under love's

"I HAD PUT ON LOVE'S HEADPHONES SO I COULD HEAR ONLY WHAT I WANTED TO HEAR, IGNORING THE TRAIN'S LOUD HORN, ITS FINAL WARNING DEVICE."

influence. I had put on love's blinders that blocked the flashing red lights warning me that a train was coming. I had put on love's headphones so I could hear only what I wanted to hear, ignoring the train's loud horn, its final warning device. I was determined to cross the railroad tracks, only to be struck from the side by the moving train of betrayal.

So I stood there smiling and trying to keep my composure. But after the last note was played and the last "I'm sorry" was spoken, I realized it was time for me to face my destiny. I dreaded taking that long walk back up the church aisle. I had dreamed that my new bride would be there to accompany me. But now I had to make this walk alone.

Once I passed the last church pew, I looked back one last time before I pulled on the brass door handle opening the ten-foot maple wood door. The burst of light from outside temporarily blinded me. I blocked the sunrays with the back of my hand before I took my first step into the rest of life. I paused for a moment, looking around to see if any of the guests were still there. I just wanted to be alone. I took a seat at the top of the concrete steps and looked out over the church's parking lot, staring into my mind's eye. It was at that moment that I began to reflect on how I found myself in this place. "Why me?" I yelled before dropping my head into the palms of my hands.

I couldn't hold back the tears any longer. I thought about all the things I could have or should have done differently to avoid this feeling of emptiness inside of me. But what else was there to do? I had done all that I could do to convey my love for her. It was difficult to digest that my best wasn't good enough. But then I began to hear in my head the sinister voices of women I had deceived over the years. They were saying things like, "You are going to get yours one day." And, "You are wrong, Mark. Just watch and see. Your turn will come." I had finally reaped what I had sown.

After temporarily bandaging my heart's internal bleeding, I mustered enough strength to drive myself home. In my car, I had the CD player queued up to play the song my bride-to-be and I had picked to take us back down memory lane and to remind us of this day for the rest of our lives. I quickly hit the FM button on the car's radio in order to avoid the floodgate of tears bound to be opened again. Once I reached the house that we were together going to call home and I opened the front door, memories of the past 30-plus years hit me simultaneously. I had pictures of the two of us as kids growing up together displayed around the room, as well as recent portraits taken of us draped all over the living room walls.

Over the next few weeks my home became my prison, isolating me from the rest of the world. I didn't want to hear, "It's going to be all right," from another person. And the words, "God has something better in store for you," or, "It's best it happened now instead of a couple months later," just didn't seem to make sense. I questioned God's mercy and why He would allow this to happen to me.

One evening, while watching television—alone—the phone rang. I checked the caller ID and saw that it was Mr. Rodgers, one of the few men that I loved, admired and respected. He just happened to be the father of the woman who caused me all of my pain.

He called to tell me that my ex-fiancée had just married another man. Not only that, he went on to explain that his daughter had resumed a relationship with a man from her past while we were engaged. "What?" I said as the muscles in my hand relaxed causing the phone to fall to the floor. My heart skipped beats. Not one beat…but three! I could hear Mr. Rodgers calling my name through the phone's receiver.

"Mark...Mark." I picked the phone up from the floor and listened to the excuses he made about why he didn't say anything to me about this sooner and how he felt he should be the one to tell me about it now. He provided me with more words of encouragement before finally ending this troubling call.

Now, all the hopes of her calling me to say she had made a mistake vanished. For weeks I tried to heal myself through self-talk and busy work, but my heart was hurting even more and my masculinity felt challenged. So I did what any man would do in a situation like this. I went out to popular hot spots looking for a woman to help me take my mind off of my troubles. I called Tammy. I called Rochelle. And I called up Carmen. All old girlfriends whom I had already known intimately and whom I thought would provide a smooth transition back to single life. But what happened was just the opposite. Although the times would pass and I would feel better for a while, I would still find myself speaking about my love for my ex-fiancée. Every woman I brought into my inner circle would inevitably become burdened with my tears and sad stories and find me to be a big disappointment. Instead of them dealing with a man they could enjoy, what they found was a man lost in his own sorrow. I was like a beautifully wrapped box placed underneath the Christmas tree, with no gift inside.

That following Monday on my way to work, I stopped my car at a gas station to refuel. Standing there pumping my gas, an older man wearing a pair of dusty blue jeans and a dingy white shirt unexpectedly stopped and asked me, "Do you know Jesus?"

"Of course," I said, taken aback, but then he asked another question. "Then why are you running from Him?" I looked at the old man with uncertainty. *What is he talking about? How can he say that to me? He doesn't know me. I was born and raised in the church.* I politely brushed him off and returned the nozzle to the pump before getting back in my car to head to work.

But sitting at my desk, I pondered the old man's question for the rest of that day. Why am I running from Him? My mind began to think back to those nights when I woke up in a cold sweat with dreams of running and running, not knowing why I was running or who I was running from. Just running.

The first eighteen years of my life were spent preparing me to lead my father's church. The last fifteen were spent destroying the vision that he had for my life. My father was the minister of a church that he built from a small membership group in our living room to one of the city's most prominent churches. I would spend many hours researching and studying the Bible and helping him prepare his lessons and sermons, and it soon became the assumption that I would follow in his footsteps. His guidance through the Scriptures was his way of preparing me to do just that.

But after graduating from high school and accepting a basketball scholarship that took me away from home, I soon discovered a life very

"THEN WHY ARE YOU RUNNING FROM HIM?"

different from the one I had always known. I began to explore things that my father would consider sinful, such as drinking, clubbing and sleeping with several women at a time. And to avoid the continuous harassment from my peers, I abandoned my religious beliefs and seldom picked up a Bible again.

The new life felt good. I enjoyed the freedom and the ability to do what I wanted with what appeared to be no consequence or no harm. For the first time in my life, I had the freedom to make my own choices, and my choices were made

"THE FIRST EIGHTEEN YEARS OF MY LIFE WERE SPENT PREPARING ME TO LEAD MY FATHER'S CHURCH. THE LAST FIFTEEN WERE SPENT DESTROYING THE VISION THAT HE HAD FOR MY LIFE."

based on one thing and one thing alone…what felt good to me at the time. I was no longer looked upon as the preacher's son and no longer used the Bible to make decisions. Yes…the new life felt good. But what I did not realize was that those days were the beginning of a fifteen-year lifestyle that would ultimately crack the very foundation that my father had worked so hard to build.

My heart still ached from not knowing what I had done

wrong in the eyes of my ex-fiancée or why she no longer loved me. But now I pondered the many things I had done wrong in the eyes of my fathers....both heavenly and earthly. I wondered now if they even still loved me.

I tried everything to bring closure to this chapter in my

> ## "I BEGAN TO EXPLORE THINGS THAT MY FATHER WOULD CONSIDER SINFUL, SUCH AS DRINKING, CLUBBING AND SLEEPING WITH SEVERAL WOMEN AT A TIME."

life, to move passed the pain. But it was not until I allowed my heavenly Father to take the leading role and began to have serious conversations with Him that I truly began to move forward in my life. He comforted me and gave me strength, and that's when my true healing began.

I have since vowed never to cause a woman the pain that I experienced, and this book is a step in keeping true to my vow. As I wrote each word of this book, I felt the pain of the hearts I manipulated over the years being finally lifted from me. I felt the weight of guilt that I have been carrying around over the years being relinquished from my soul.

So you see, I speak from a perspective of experience from both sides of the game. Through my personal tragedy, I have seen the error of my ways and turned away from them. I have grown in many ways during the years after my devastating break-up and have survived a truly difficult period in my life. In sharing my story, I hope to help others see that God has always been there, calling out to them. He has and will continue to use their heartaches to bring them close to Him. He used this experience to mold me into the man He wanted me to be.

"I HAVE SINCE VOWED NEVER TO CAUSE A WOMAN THE PAIN THAT I EXPERIENCED."

I hope that this book will particularly help strengthen women and give them a new understanding of the men they love and provide them more of the tools they need to play the game of love and relationships on a more even playing field. I want to give women the chance to be the ones to shout, "Checkmate," and not always settle for being the ones who are checked. The pages of this book are written like the pages of the rule book. And the stories will show you the practical illustrations of how they apply to the men who fall into the category of the man I used to be.

In addition, I want to give men whose manhood has been beaten down by a situation similar to mine hope that there is a light at the end of the tunnel. I want the men to understand that there is a different definition of manhood besides what society has classified manhood to be. I hope the stories inside of this book will magnify how a man's actions can negatively or positively impact the lives of women.

1

CHAPTER ONE
RECOGNIZING A PLAYER

So that you can to understand the mentality of a man who fits the profile of a player, it is necessary to define the term in the context of how it is used here. For the purpose of this discussion, a player is a man who has several sexual partners but is not committed to any one of them. One may also think of a player as a man who is able to carry on relationships with several women simultaneously.

There may be other descriptions for a player, but the common denominator in all of them is that a player is involved with more than one woman at a time, on some level.

While players come in a variety of ages, socio-economic backgrounds, and levels of expertise, typically they have a few common characteristics. They are charismatic, personable, and, at the same time, very private and mysterious. No one can

WHAT ARE THE TELLTALE SIGNS THAT A MAN MIGHT BE A PLAYER?

say with any certainty what is true about this kind of man's social life, other than that he knows quite a few people and moves in a few different social circles.

So then, what are the telltale signs that a man might be a player? Let's say you meet a man, and after having an in-depth conversation with your friends about him, you are then alone with your own thoughts. Your conversation with yourself might go something like this: "I like the fact that he's able to communicate his feelings towards me. He calls me several times a day. I know that he cares about me because he sends cards and flowers. It's the little things that he does."

I would guess that you would agree that this man's actions are a good measure of his character. After all, most of us have been taught that actions speak louder than words, and we live by that rule. But, should a man's actions be the sole indicator of his intentions? I would argue that actions alone are an insufficient measure of a man's intent. In addition to considering a man's actions, it is imperative that his words be given the

SHOULD A MAN'S ACTIONS BE THE SOLE INDICATOR OF HIS INTENTIONS?

same scrutiny. Because if a man's words and actions are in opposition, beware, he might be a player.

Fundamentally, a player's words and actions line up as follows:

1. **All talk and no action.** For example, he will talk about the two of you together in a committed relationship, but when the time comes for him to step up to the plate, he can't be found.

2. **All action and little talk.** For example, he calls you every day of the week, and when the weekend comes, he picks you up and takes you to dinner and a movie, just showering you with attention. But when the time comes for him to commit himself, he's full of excuses as to why he can't settle down right now.

3. **A lot of talk and a lot of action.** For example, he shares his dreams with you and makes sure that all the time you spend together is very special, but take notice. He never specifically says that he wants to live out his dreams with *you*.

These examples summarize how players generally behave. Once again, when a man's actions and words are not aligned, he may be a player.

There are some secrets that men vow never to reveal, so read on to let the truth be told.

2

CHAPTER TWO
THE PLAYERS' CLUB

There are some secrets men vow never to give up. This is the unspoken code of the "Players' Club." "The Players' Club? What is that?" you might ask. The "Players' Club" is where men fine tune their existing skills, create new strategies, and exchange success stories. Of course, there is no physical building called the "Players' Club." "The Players' Club" is more an informal gathering of men who meet in places where they can fraternize—a locker room or a barbershop, for example. Since women do not possess what is required for admission, I am providing exclusive access via my expe-

NOT ALL PLAYERS PLAY THE GAME WITH THE SAME LEVEL OF FINESSE.

riences.

Not all players play the game with the same level of finesse. Three key skill levels will be explained within the next few chapters. As in most games, talent varies. In addition to explaining what each kind of player does, I will also suggest what women can do to counteract the strategies that are used by their male counterparts. After reading this book, you will have a good understanding of how the game is played and a great reference for future use.

Hold on for the ride. It's going to get bumpy.

3

CHAPTER THREE
THE OBJECTIVE

A player's intent, in most cases, is to fulfill his physical and monetary desires. Most men will say or do virtually anything to satisfy his sexual and financial appetite. And he accomplishes his objectives by making a few strategic moves. For example, a man will get in touch with his feminine side. How does he do this? He masks his desire for sex and money behind acts of kindness and signs of sensitivity.

The first strategy in reaching his long-term objective is to get a woman to be committed to a casual, sexual relationship without requiring any level of commitment from him. Men know that this arrangement is possible, so they begin by making the moves towards getting a woman in bed the first time. If they are successful once, they know the game is halfway over.

A man will then begin to establish a commitment-free

A MAN WILL THEN BEGIN TO ESTABLISH A COMMITMENT-FREE SEXUAL RELATIONSHIP WITH A WOMAN BY MAKING HER FEEL SO COMFORTABLE WITH THE ARRANGEMENT THAT HE CAN CALL HER AT HIS CONVENIENCE—BE IT MORNING, NOON, OR NIGHT.

sexual relationship with a woman by making her feel so comfortable with the arrangement that he can call her at his convenience—be it morning, noon, or night. Men are selfish creatures by nature and see no problem in having a woman, or women, available to them when they feel the urge to be amorous. This will make life more convenient for them as the game progresses.

The Principle of Fair Exchange

From a male's perspective, one good turn deserves another. Let's examine the principle called "fair exchange." Fair exchange, in the mind of a man, is essentially trading favors. Men who fit the player profile do not see an issue with expecting sex in return for dinner and a movie or asking for a loan to pay his rent for the month in exchange for a couple of well-planned evenings. For an example, when a man offers to purchase a drink in a club, he does so with the expectation that he will at least have a conversation in exchange for the drink. And, with that conversation, his proverbial foot is in the door.

This starts the game. And after his "bishop" has captured one of the woman's "pawns" (i.e., after you all have had sex for the first time), he begins to work on the mind of the woman in an attempt to control it.

Women have been conditioned to believe that if a man knows nothing else, he knows that he wants sex. Is that all that men want? No. Is that the only thing on a man's mind? No. A man who fits the player profile does think about sex, but that's not all he wants.

He wants control. He wants control of her body. He wants control of her money. He wants control of her mind. He wants control of the board. He wants control.

Women have also been led to think that the game starts with the first phone call and somehow ends after sex. That is ridiculously far from the truth. It's often only after she has been intimate with him that the games really begin. It then becomes the time when she should be on guard. And her guard should be as high as a level "orange" on the national security alert.

Then the man decides his next move. If the sex is gratifying, he will make another diagonal move with his bishop, and the woman's king is in the dangerous position of check. He is now ready to reap the rewards from his investment, and the game is almost over.

At this point, women will usually give men the benefit of the doubt and tell themselves things such as, "I know he is seeing other women, but he will stop once he gets to know me." Or they may say, "He has some good qualities, so I should just hold on." And, if the sex is good, she may even rationalize that that is enough. Now her guard is down, she never even sounded an "alert," and her heart is left open and unprotected. Her king is in check by his bishop. She looks to find all her king's escape routes only to discover that all squares are covered. CHECKMATE!

Now she is faced with only the options of proceeding with the "game" and somehow developing a healthy relationship against the odds…or just letting go. Her emotions are fueling her decisions and, now that sex is no longer the allure, she seeks to find other things such as gifts and items of monetary value as an alternative to win his attention. Game over.

SHE LOOKS TO FIND ALL HER KING'S ESCAPE ROUTES ONLY TO DISCOVER THAT ALL SQUARES ARE COVERED. CHECKMATE!

Men, however, see this time as the golden opportunity to take advantage of the woman and the casual sexual relationship he has established. Without any commitments, he is free to exploit her vulnerability for his gain...his sexual gain...his financial gain. And his control of the game.

4

CHAPTER FOUR
MEN 101: THINGS WOMEN MUST UNDERSTAND

Women must understand and accept some funda-
mental facts about men. First, a man only does
what he wants to do and only when he is ready.
Second, a man will settle down when the good Lord places it
on his heart to do so. This will happen only when his con-
science tells him that it is time.

There is virtually nothing a woman can say or do to
change these facts. Think about it. How many times has any
man you've known changed what he says or does based on how
good a woman has been to him? When have a woman's actions
prevented a man from coming home late? Or made him return
phone calls? Or made him keep his word? It doesn't happen.

If you have not figured it out, men make conscious decisions to enjoy themselves. They do what they want and worry about the consequences later. When a man decides to do whatever it is he intends to do, a "woman's worth" is often not on his mind. From most men's perspectives, if the only consequence of satisfying whatever urge he has is to have to hear a few hours of complaining, it's worth it.

A man expects that a woman will accept whatever explanation he gives. And if all else fails, then he will play his trump card, because he knows it has worked in the past. What is the trump card? The trump card is some type of weakness she has

FROM MOST MEN'S PERSPECTIVE, IF THE ONLY CONSEQUENCE OF SATISFYING WHATEVER URGE HE HAS IS TO HAVE TO HEAR A FEW HOURS OF COMPLAINING, IT'S WORTH IT.

for him, whether it is his sex, his tears, or his use of the words "I love you." He will use this only when he knows he has messed up or is about to lose her. It is after the woman calms down that the games begin again.

Men tell each other all about how the woman ranted and raved. The response is usually the same: "Man, I just stood there without saying anything back to her so I wouldn't trip up and have to explain where, when, and with whom I did what I did. I was prepared to tell her I loved her if I had to. When she finally realized I was not going to say anything, she gave up." While the woman is going through a range of emotions, screaming at him and calling him every name in the book, he is still focused on the fact that he got away with whatever he did.

This leads me to the next point. Too often, a woman tries to prove to a man that she is the woman he needs. The truth is that no matter how complete she is or is not, a man is not going to settle down unless he is ready. Forget the extravagant dinners, the expensive gifts, the money that was loaned (another gift), not to mention the special sexual favors. You know the ones: late night sex, early morning sex, oral sex, and yes, anal sex. (Be real for a minute. Men always want a

A MAN IS NOT GOING TO SETTLE DOWN UNLESS HE IS READY.

little more than they've had in the past. When men hear that their friends are engaging in anal sex, they want a chance to experience the same thing. These new acts are not about a man's sexuality. That is another topic for another book. But men expect a woman to try new and different sexual experiences for them. Just because a man wants to have anal sex does not mean he is bisexual. However, I would think twice about a brother seeking those types of sexual favors. So keep your radar detectors in working order.)

I hate to be the bearer of bad news, but there is no amount of work a woman can do that will make this kind of man worth her effort. Until he decides to change, he will do only what he wants to do, including committing to a woman or not.

I am not telling women to give up hope. But just know that you cannot look good enough, cook well enough, be rich enough, or love a man enough to make this kind of man do what he is not ready to do.

5

CHAPTER FIVE
SKILL LEVEL I:
MR. WONDERFUL

The majority of men who are players fit into the first category explained earlier—men who are "all talk and no action." This man is the easiest to figure out, because his type is the most common. If a woman pays attention to the signs, his intentions will be evident within a few weeks.

A master with words, this man has the uncanny ability to convince women that ice isn't cold or the sun isn't hot. He will make you question the things you know and not question the things you don't. He is able to convince almost any woman that he is kind, giving, and trustworthy. By the time this smooth talker persuades a woman to go out with him, she believes he is sensitive and generous—an all-around good person. This man is so good at winning the confidence of others that he believes his ability to talk will get him into any relationship he desires. His actions, however, are another story.

Even though he has verbally expressed every romantic thought he could think of and has spent some time with a woman, he is more likely to be found in a nightclub every weekend instead of being with her. That is, unless he is horny

A MASTER WITH WORDS, THIS MAN HAS THE UNCANNY ABILITY TO CONVINCE WOMEN THAT ICE ISN'T COLD OR THE SUN ISN'T HOT. HE WILL MAKE YOU QUESTION THE THINGS YOU KNOW AND NOT QUESTION THE THINGS YOU DON'T.

on a weekend night. He may appear to be sacrificing a night with the fellas to be with her, but his need for sex is more than likely the reason he has chosen to stay in for the evening.

An encounter with this kind of player may happen something like this…meet Derrick Jones.

6

CHAPTER SIX
DERRICK JONES

It is Friday night at a popular spot in the city. The music is nice, the crowd is just right. Everyone is having a great time. In a corner of the club, a group of attractive women stand together profiling. In the distance, a group of men peer in the direction of these women. The standout of the men's group has set his sights on one of the women whom he finds attractive. She has also noticed him. She knows that he is checking her out, because she just saw his friends try to sneak-a-peek.

He approaches her very confidently, because in his mind he is the Mack, a platinum card-carrying player. He is sure that she is noticing how well-groomed he is. He is clean-shaven, has a nice haircut, and a bright smile. His off-the-rack suit fits nicely, and his shoes are polished. Once he reaches her, he extends his manicured hand but stands close enough to make sure she can smell his trendy cologne. What she does not see is the condom he is carrying in his wallet, because he is ready for anything tonight.

He introduces himself as "Derrick," and she responds by giving her name. Derrick notices that she already has a drink;

WHAT SHE DOES NOT SEE IS THE CONDOM HE IS CARRYING IN HIS WALLET, BECAUSE HE IS READY FOR ANYTHING TONIGHT.

actually, he notices that her glass is half full. To seem like a gentleman, he asks if she would like something to drink. He is sure that she will say no because she already has one.

He then glances over his shoulder to see if the fellas are watching; they are and give him a nod. This is confirmation that he is on his game. You see, Derrick is "the man" in the eyes of his friends. They are just giving him "props." It would be a player disaster to be dismissed by a lady in front of the fellas.

Having seen all the movies and read all the books on how to be a player, he feels he is the Chosen One, the man with the golden tongue, the man who is able to "talk" a woman into anything.

The two are engaged in a superficial conversation when

the DJ plays a popular song. Derrick senses that she likes the song and asks her to dance. She accepts, and they head toward the dance floor. On the way, he is stopped twice by different women who say hello. Derrick sees this as a plus, because he believes his new friend will think that other women see something in him. He earns some credibility by introducing her to them. Four songs later, he leads her to a cozy booth where they continue to talk. He does not ask if she would like another drink and ignores his own thirst.

While the conversation continues, several men and women stop over and speak to Derrick. Of course, Derrick's new friend is curious as to who this man really is. Why would he know so many people? At this point, she does not realize that Derrick is a club-junkie. Seldom does he miss a Friday night.

Before long, Derrick has gotten her phone number and promises to call her. Before they can finish conversing, one of his friends motions toward him as if to say, "Come over here." Derrick excuses himself and again promises to call soon. Before he walks away, he tells her to save a dance for him, if it is not too much to ask.

> AT THIS POINT, SHE DOES NOT REALIZE THAT DERRICK IS A CLUB-JUNKIE. SELDOM DOES HE MISS A FRIDAY NIGHT.

Both of them return to their friends, and in no time at all, Derrick is working the club again. Since this new lady has a nice body and looks like she has some money in the bank, he does not want to mess up the opportunity. So he limits the number of women he spends any time with, because he knows that she's watching.

The DJ makes the last call for alcohol, and Derrick looks down at his watch to check the time. The bar will be closing soon, and he wants to make one final impression. To make sure that she sees him before leaving, he stands near the exit doors. When he spots her walking towards the ladies' room, he calls out to her. She turns around to see who is calling her name. They approach each other and he asks, "What happened to my dance?" She's flattered and explains that she didn't forget, but she did not see him when the good songs were playing.

After seeing her in the light of the hallway, his eyes light up and the words, "Damn! I didn't know you were that fine," escape from his mouth. He explains that he was merely giving her a compliment. She smiles and tells him that she has to run and hopes to speak with him soon. He offers to see her to her car. She accepts and tells her friends to call her when they get home. Once at her car, he makes small talk for a couple of minutes then grabs her hand and kisses it gently before telling her to drive safely.

She gets in her car and drives away. He knows that he has made a lasting impression; the kiss on the hand was a brilliant move. Now that she is gone, he finds his friends, and they do

NOW THAT SHE IS GONE, HE FINDS HIS FRIENDS, AND THEY DO A LITTLE PLP (PARKING-LOT PIMP) FOR A BIT.

a little PLP (parking-lot pimp) for a bit. For those of you who do not recognize the term, a "parking-lot pimp" drives around the parking lot of an establishment several times before leaving for the night.

He drops off his friend who was riding along, then checks the time. It is after 2:00 a.m. He assumes that his new friend has made it home, so he calls her to make sure. Of course, he is working his plan. You see, this call is a test of two things. First, to see how she will react to receiving a call during the wee hours of the morning and, second, to see how she reacts to his offer to stop by her place for breakfast. Her reactions will tell him all he needs to know.

She answers, as he hoped she would, and he goes to work. Her reaction to the first test is good. He knows this because she answered the call and her mood is happy. After he asks if she made it home safely, he jokingly asks if she would like him to stop by for breakfast. He does not know what to expect but needs to know if she is open to the offer. Her response will determine how he proceeds.

If he has no success that morning, Derrick will attempt to call her a few hours later, around nine or ten o'clock. He has to test the waters to get a feel for where he stands. He is hoping she will allow him to take her out or, better yet, allow him to come over to her house and bypass the going out and spending money thing. He is feeling horny and would be willing to give up this Saturday night to get a piece. If not, he will be back out tonight prowling for someone else.

Her telephone rings and she answers with a "Hello."

"Hi, this is Derrick, the guy from last night at the club. Did I wake you up?"

"No."

"I have been thinking about you ever since I met you last night. I really had fun dancing with you. I saw you when you first walked in the club. I said to myself, who is that woman? You were looking good in those jeans. I wanted to see what you had planned for today. Hopefully, we can spend some time together."

"I don't know right now, Derrick. I have some errands to run, and I'm not sure what time I'll be finished."

"Tell you what. Why don't you call me when you finish with your errands, and we can stop off and grab some take-out. I have a couple of new releases from Blockbuster we can watch."

Derrick's success or failure at reaching his objective hinges on the choice the woman makes. She is in control at this point. Derrick knows it. He hopes that after spending what he called quality time with her in the club last night, it will lead to an easy night of sex tonight, but so far the jury is still out. If she is to remain in control, she should not be eager to accept an outing with Derrick so soon. But if she does go out with him, she needs to make sure it is out somewhere instead of to his house or hers. He wants to take the cheap way out, so he doesn't have to invest more money than he has to. He will not talk about going out but will try to convince her to stay home and watch movies or something. If he does take her out, he will be looking for a return on his investment in the forms of loans or gifts.

He is all talk, and to counter his attack, she must be prepared to overlook his conversational skill and focus on his actions and what kind of actions. It seems that he has actions, but they are not the ones that lead to a commitment with her. Instead, they will give the appearance of emotional intimacy through sexual intimacy. If he is unsuccessful with sexing her with no commitment, he will even go to the extreme of offering to be in a relationship with her in order to develop her into a casual sexual partner. His conversation will be along the lines of making her his Boo, main squeeze, or his girlfriend. This scenario will continue to happen basically the same way in the days and weeks to come. When this story ends, either he will have added a new woman to his collection or he will have been sent on his way. It all depends on whether she will eventually see the disconnect between his words and his actions.

7

CHAPTER SEVEN
SKILL LEVEL II:
MR. SENSITIVE

Let's take a look at men who have moved to a higher skill level. This type of man will demonstrate his interest in a particular woman, but he will never commit. He is also more capable of convincing a woman to enter into a casual sexual relationship. He accomplishes his objective by virtue of what he is willing to do with a woman and for her. His approach to getting his way is different from the type of man described in the previous chapters. What is consistent, however, is that his words and actions are still in opposition.

There are a couple of distinctions between a player in the previous category and one on skill level two. At skill level two, a man pursues a different class of women and realizes that he must improve his game in order to meet and ultimately manip-

MEN AT SKILL LEVEL TWO ARE
SERIOUS CONTENDERS. THEY
HAVE DONE THEIR HOMEWORK:
THEY HAVE QUIZZED THEIR
FEMALE FRIENDS TO FIND OUT
WHAT MAKES WOMEN TICK;
THEY KEEP UP WITH CURRENT
TRENDS, LIKE THE LATEST
CUISINE OR THE CURRENT ART
EXHIBIT; AND THEY ARE
CULTURED AND WELL-READ.
THEY HAVE GAINED INSIGHT
INTO WOMEN'S PSYCHES BY
WATCHING TALK SHOWS AND
READING BOOKS OR MAGAZINES.

ulate them. Unlike the character "Derrick," the next character is less transparent.

Men at skill level two are serious contenders. They have done their homework: they have quizzed their female friends to find out what makes women tick; they keep up with current trends, like the latest cuisine or the current art exhibit; and they are cultured and well-read. They have gained insight into women's psyches by watching talk shows and reading books or magazines. They have gotten in touch with their sensitive sides. They have also sought advice from seasoned men like uncles, older brothers, and older friends.

This type of man is more skillful in the presence of a woman than often his blue-collar skilled comrades. He does not frequent hot spots where the crowds consist of young people of the same race and age. Rather, he patronizes establishments that cater to a mixed clientele—mixed in terms of their ages, ethnicities, and income levels. He pursues any woman who fits his criteria, regardless of her race or ethnicity. This man is likely to have a nucleus of women that he enjoys spending time with, but not one that he would take home to mom.

Every man believes that his game is on point and that, given the right opportunity, he can get any woman he wants. But a man on this level has convinced himself that he cannot lose. He approaches his craft from a variety of angles, including, but not limited to, wining and dining a woman in exclusive restaurants, inviting her to events sponsored by his employer, inviting her to social func-

EVERY MAN BELIEVES THAT HIS GAME IS ON POINT AND THAT, GIVEN THE RIGHT OPPORTUNITY, HE CAN GET ANY WOMAN HE WANTS.

tions among his friends, and even inviting her to church. He is hoping all of these outings will have a positive influence on her decision-making process. It may not be apparent to her in the beginning, but these outings are more for her benefit than his. The truth of the matter is she plays a big part in his success at playing the game. She does not realize it, though, because he is so clever.

How can he be so skillful? To begin, he is willing to do what it takes to make a woman believe that there is a potential relationship in the works. In actuality, nothing is further from the truth. This man is putting on the same show for as many women as he can. He has prepared an arsenal of answers to questions about where the relationship is heading and whether the relationship is exclusive.

She might hear him say something like this: "I am not ready for a relationship right now because I have been hurt before. I was really hurt by her; and I am just afraid of being hurt again,"...Translation...I am not ready for a relationship because I am still looking for that special someone, but I do want to sleep with you until I find that special someone. But we all know that line wouldn't work.

And then there is the "I am focusing on my future right now. I have a couple of business ventures I am working on, and I won't have much free time in the near future" excuse....Translation...I am really a buster...my car is about to be repossessed...I can barely make ends meet, but hopefully you will repay the money I spent on us going out tonight, or I have a lot going on and the only thing I want from you right now is sex.

This type of deception began as soon as he said, "Hello." Watch him at work.

8

CHAPTER EIGHT
MICHAEL YOUNG

It is Wednesday around noon, and Michael Young has decided to go out for lunch. He chooses a nearby restaurant where he knows there will be no shortage of women. Michael is on the hunt for a new opponent.

While he waits to be seated, a group of women walks through the entrance doors, one of whom he finds attractive. He takes a step back to capture a full view of her. He looks at her face, her legs, and, of course, her booty. Just as he is taking a second look at her booty, the hostess calls his name to be seated. Not for one moment do his eyes move away from her. He wonders where she and her friends will be seated. He begins to think about how he will approach her. He takes a seat, peruses the menu, and waits to place his lunch order. As he is placing his order, he notices that the group of women has been seated three tables away. Perfect! He will time his exit so that he will be leaving around the same time they are.

About half-an-hour later, Michael asks for his check. He has made sure that he will be at the exit doors a few steps ahead of the group of women. He plans to open the door for them—and hopefully make eye contact with his prospective opponent. As they approach the door, Michael says, "Let me get that for you all." At the same time, he looks directly at the lady with whom he would like to connect. Ironically, she is the only one who looks back at him. In a very soft voice she says, "Thank you." Michael takes the opportunity to strike up a conversation.

"No problem. How are you today?"

"Fine, and yourself?" she replies.

"Pretty good. Just on my way back to work. By the way, my name is Michael Young. May I ask your name?"

"Jasmine Carter," she responds.

"Jasmine. What a pretty name. I realize that you should be on your way, and I don't want to waste your time, but I would like to speak with you later and was wondering if you have a business card or a number where I can reach you?" As he is speaking, he retrieves a business card holder from his pocket. He removes two business cards. The extra card is just in case Jasmine does not have one of her own. In that case, he will ask her to write down her contact number.

"Here's my information," he says and gives the cards to her.

THE GAMES MEN PLAY

It turns out that she has a business card, which she gives to him. He mentions that he has a meeting to attend and politely excuses himself. As he makes his way back toward his office, he has already begun to plan his next move. He gives himself a pat on the back for the successful series of events that he has just engineered. He will call Jasmine in about an hour. She will have settled back into work by then.

Jasmine's phone rings and Michael says, "Hello, this is Michael Young. We met this afternoon."

The reception she gives him will determine the direction in which he leads the conversation. If she is warm, he will continue the conversation with insignificant chatter, so as not to get into a deep conversation. She is receptive, so he reels her in. He tells her that he respects the fact that she is at work and asks if he can call her at home later. She thanks him and gives him her home phone number.

Thinking strategically, Michael calls her that evening around 7:30 p.m. He figures that by this time she will be home but will not have eaten dinner. When she answers the phone, her mood is good. It gives him the confidence he needs to ask her to meet him for dinner. He asks and she accepts. They agree to meet at a popular local Italian restaurant.

He arrives a few minutes early so that he can get familiar with the staff and the restaurant. He also looks over the menu so that he can order intelligently and to make sure he can cover the cost of dinner.

Jasmine arrives fashionably late, but she apologizes anyway. Michael doesn't mind; he used the extra time to memorize the names of the waitstaff—he wants Jasmine to think that he eats in this restaurant frequently. The waiter addresses Michael by name and asks if he will have his usual drink. Michael answers, "Sure." He is banking on Jasmine being impressed. Then he suggests a drink for her to try and she agrees.

HE WANTS TO LEARN AS MUCH AS POSSIBLE ABOUT HER SO HE CAN USE SOME OF HER LIKES OR DISLIKES AGAINST HER.

The night is progressing as Michael planned. He believes that he has scored points for being well-known in the restaurant and being able to suggest a drink. He decides that it is time to find out what Jasmine is all about. He wants to learn as much as possible about her so he can use some of her likes or dislikes against her.

Michael is hoping a subject will pique Jasmine's interest and she will open up. Unlike Derrick, who is all talk, Michael wants to talk as little as possible so he can learn about her.

The meal arrives. They eat and continue talking throughout the main course, dessert and coffee. From Michael's perspective, the evening has been a success, so he begins the process of ending the outing. He looks at his watch to check the time. He does not want Jasmine to think he is looking for anything tonight other than dinner and good company, so he tells her that it is getting late and suggests that they leave.

"Look at the time! I have an early start tomorrow," he says. She responds that she does as well, and they prepare to leave.

The entire evening, from beginning to end, is a well-planned scheme that Michael has used on numerous occasions. This is his way of appearing to be a gentleman who is grounded, enjoys great food and great company, and respects a woman by ending the night at a decent hour. Most of the time his plan works like a charm. This evening is no exception.

While he is driving home, he calls Jasmine from his cell phone. He thanks her for taking the time to meet him for dinner. He also tells her that he enjoyed the evening and hopes to speak with her the next day.

After he is home and lying in bed, he begins to work on his strategy in his mind. The focus of the game at this point is to take Jasmine as fast as he can. He wants her to make decisions based on her emotions about him instead of the logic that might raise suspicions.

He will get inside her mind by spending as much time with her as possible within a short period of time. He wants Jasmine to become emotionally attached to him, so he will spend countless hours with her, including holding long conversations by phone. The result, Michael hopes, will be to increase her comfort level with him in a matter of weeks.

Friday is a couple of days away, and Michael has to prepare a plan of attack. He makes his next strategic move by calling Jasmine on Thursday morning before she gets to her office. He intentionally wants to reach her voicemail—that way he can leave a message that she will think about all day. How does he accomplish this?

Michael leaves the following message: "Hello, Jasmine, this is Michael. I know you haven't made it in to work yet, but I am on my way in to the office, and I was just thinking about last night and how much I enjoyed your company. I hope you had as much fun as I did. Talk to you soon."

Michael believes the message will catch Jasmine off guard, because she is not expecting him to call so soon. (Right hook, Ladies, and you go down for an 8 count; but you have to get up, because the fight is not over.)

Michael arrives at his office about five minutes after he leaves the message for Jasmine. He sits back in his chair with his hands crossed behind his head. He has accomplished his goal for the morning. He will be on Jasmine's mind all day or at least most of it. He will wait until she calls him back so as not to appear desperate or overbearing. He believes that he maintains control over the speed of the relationship by waiting for Jasmine to call him back. (Can this be called a relationship yet?)

Almost like clockwork, only a few hours pass before Jasmine calls him back. After three rings he answers with a deep voice.

"Hello, this is Michael Young."

She hesitates for a moment, then says, "Hello, Michael, this is Jasmine. Did I catch you at a bad time?"

"Of course not. It's always nice to hear your voice. I do have a meeting in about ten minutes, but I can talk to you for a minute or two."

He will not reference the message he left for her that morning because he wants her to bring it up first. He stays in control by not mentioning it.

"Thank you for the thoughtful message this morning. I also had a nice time last night," Jasmine says.

"I'm glad you had a good time," Michael replies. "I don't mean to rush you off the phone, but I have to get ready for my meeting. Hey, if you don't have any plans for Friday night, I have a pair of tickets for a play this weekend and would love for you to join me. I'll give you a call tonight, and we can discuss it."

Jasmine replies, "I understand you have to go. Let me quickly check my schedule. I am free on Friday night, so is it a date?"

Michael is uncomfortable with Jasmine's reference to a date. He disregards the question and tells her, "I'll call you tonight, and we can sort out the details."

It's Thursday night around 10:30 p.m., and Jasmine's phone rings.

"Hello, Jaz, this is Michael. I hope I didn't wake you up. I apologize for calling so late."

"That's all right, Michael. I had just gotten into bed."

"I won't keep you too long. I was calling to make sure that you are still going to accompany me to the play tomorrow night."

"Of course," Jasmine replies. There is a hint of excitement in her voice.

Michael then gives her an option to meet him there or be picked up. Jasmine chooses to meet him at the theater.

"The play starts at 8:00 p.m. Meet me at 7:30 p.m. in front of the theater," Michael suggests.

Jasmine replies, "I'll see you then."

They say goodbye and agree to speak the next day, which is Friday. Michael hangs up the phone and walks into the kitchen to get himself a bottle of beer. He was hoping to call late enough on Thursday to ensure Jasmine had been thinking about him all evening and putting her plans for Friday on hold until she heard from him. While twisting the top off, he can't help but think what a calculated move he had made tonight.

Michael laughs to himself. He wants to take her as fast as he can. So Friday night, a normal date night, seems harmless to her. With the weekend approaching, he is banking on two or three more outings with her within a five-day period.

Friday morning rolls around, and Jasmine strolls into the office. She notices the red light blinking, indicating she has messages. Hoping that one of those messages will be Michael, she picks up the receiver and presses message retrieval. At the same time the phone rings. (Could this be? Could it be

Michael?) Not wanting to seem excited, she lets the phone ring a couple more times before answering, "This is Jasmine."

"Hey, Jaz girl, what's up?" Her girlfriends are calling to see what the plans are for Friday night. "So what's up for tonight? I heard this new band will be performing at Visions. How about it?"

"Sorry, girls, I already have plans for tonight, but keep me posted on where you are, because you never know—my plans may fall through."

"Sure thing. We'll call you later."

Michael walks into his office and closes the door. He has eight hours to find the best seats in the house for the play.

REMEMBER, A MAN WILL DECIDE HOW MUCH TIME AND MONEY HE IS GOING TO INVEST IN A WOMAN TO GET HER INTO BED WHEN HE FIRST MEETS HER.

Since it is last minute, he knows that he will have to pay a pretty penny.

Calculating the cost of the tickets, he must now determine if Jasmine is worth the investment. (Remember, a man will decide how much time and money he is going to invest in a woman to get her into bed when he first meets her.) Michael looks at the cost of the tickets as a cost of doing business and is waiting for his payday—fair exchange.

At the same time, Jasmine is checking her messages, hoping that Michael left a message like he did yesterday.

Just the thought of his voice sends her stomach fluttering. Guess what! No message, so here comes the dilemma. Does she call, or wait to see if he calls her? Throwing caution to the wind, she picks up the phone and dials his number.

"Michael Young speaking."

"Hello, Michael. This is Jasmine."

"Hey, Jaz. What a nice surprise to hear such a lovely, soft voice first thing in the morning. I was just thinking about you."

In reality, Michael was hoping to talk to her today. Considering the cost of the tickets, he continues the conversation to gauge the level of interest and weigh the chances of sexual activity. Again, fair exchange. If he thinks his chances for sex are good, then he will try, but Michael won't try anything unless she gives him some vibes to that effect.

Jasmine states, "I'm not going to keep you. I was just calling to say have a nice day, and I am looking forward to our date tonight."

Damn, there goes that word again—date. To avoid any confusion Michael simply replies, "You have a good day, and I will see you tonight."

Michael hangs up the phone and continues working on his reports. He is in a hurry to finish so he can leave early. He needs to run by the barbershop for a haircut, and if he has time, to stop by his favorite clothing store.

He arrives at the theater on time in his new rust-colored linen suit with matching sandals. He is feeling like "The Man" right about now. He's looking good and smelling good. He takes one quick inventory, turns around and sees Jasmine lingering at the door. He takes a minute to freshen up his breath in hopes of getting a hello kiss. "You look great," Michael says,

"Thank you. You are looking handsome yourself."

"Sounds like the play is about to start. Why don't we go and find our seats?"

The evening is going well. Michael is a perfect gentleman. Making sure Jasmine is relaxed and enjoying herself, he glances at her every once in a while and gives her a little smile.

When they announce a thirty-minute intermission, Michael realizes that this is the perfect opportunity to learn more about her.

"Would you like to step outside until the end of the intermission?"

"Sure," Jasmine replies.

"Are you enjoying the play?"

"Yes, very much, and yourself?"

Michael replies in a deep Barry White voice, "I'm enjoying the company even more. May I ask you a personal question?"

Jasmine nods a bit hesitantly.

"When was your last relationship?"

"Umm, my last relationship, well, that's kind of personal. My last relationship was about two years ago," Jasmine replies.

"If you don't mind my asking, who broke up with whom? Or did you catch him cheating on you?"

By this time Jasmine is looking a little perplexed, but she replies, "Let's just say we grew apart."

Since Jasmine didn't answer exactly the way Michael would have hoped, he tries to edge more details out of her.

"You say you grew apart. Career-wise? Goals? Or you just fell out of love?"

Jasmine takes a minute to think to herself, Why is he asking me these questions? Is it possible that he feels there could be something between us and wants to learn more about me?

In response to Michael's question, Jasmine explains how the last man she dated had a lack of respect for her and her career. He didn't have any goals in life and just wanted to sit in front of the television playing PlayStation. She continues by saying that he was the type of man that found a job and was content; he didn't want to go any further in life, and, yes, he did end up cheating on her.

Jasmine thinks this would be the perfect time to turn the tables and asks the same question. "So, Michael, have you ever been in a serious relationship?" Before he can answer, an announcement floods the theater requesting everyone to return to their seats; the play is about to start. Michael is sitting there with a concerned look on his face trying to show sympathy for what Jasmine has just told him about her past experience.

At the same time, he is jumping for joy that it is time to return to their seats. He has never been in a serious relationship and wants to make sure he has all the possible avenues covered that his answer might lead to. Even though he has been asked this question before, he wants to make sure his response is tailor-made for her interest, beliefs, and goals. He will ponder the question during the rest of the play and make sure he brings it up later so as not to seem like he is trying to avoid the question.

Michael and Jasmine take their seats. Since Jasmine opened up to Michael a little bit, he is feeling confident as to the approach he should take. The play ends and Michael walks Jasmine to her car. Instead of asking her out for coffee, he hopes she will make a suggestion that will keep the night going. Jasmine is not quite ready to call it a night. She suggests that they stop by Visions. Michael is not familiar with the place so he goes to check it out because it might be a good spot to bring another one of his opponents.

Michael thinks he is going to listen to some music, but he is really going so her

EVEN THOUGH HE HAS BEEN ASKED THIS QUESTION BEFORE, HE WANTS TO MAKE SURE HIS RESPONSE IS TAILOR-MADE FOR HER INTEREST, BELIEFS, AND GOALS.

girls will see him. Jasmine knows the girls will be at Visions, and this will be the perfect opportunity to show Michael off and get her girls' thoughts about him.

Jasmine and Michael are enjoying themselves listening to music and laughing when Michael brings up the question Jasmine asked him earlier during the play's intermission.

"Hey Jasmine, you know when you asked me if I have ever been in a serious relationship?"

"Yeah, Michael."

"To be honest, I haven't. Not by any fault of mine, but over the past year I have been positioning myself to make the next step in my career. I have goals that I have set for myself and a time frame to reach them. The problem for me has been that the women I have been dating want a lot of time from me, and right now I don't have a lot to give, but I guess it is my fault. I should just take myself out of the dating pool until things slow down."

"Michael, you don't have to do that. You just haven't met the right woman who's understanding of the sacrifices you have to make in order meet your goals and dreams."

"Now that's what I mean."

At that moment the DJ plays her favorite song, "This Woman's Work" by Maxwell. Jasmine tells Michael how she listens to this CD every morning driving into work, but for the past week she can't find her CD.

As the evening progresses, she decides to call it a night. She really likes Michael and doesn't want to send him the wrong signals. Michael gives her a hug and a kiss good night on the cheek. About 20 minutes after driving off, he calls from the car just about the time she turns into the driveway. He says he just called to make sure she made it home all right and to let her know once again that he enjoyed her company. This is his last attempt to see if he can stop by. He will not ask but will wait for an invitation. From her response, he figures he is not going to get one, so he politely ends the conversation. But rest assured, he will call first thing on Saturday, around 9:30 a.m., depending on if she told him she is a late sleeper or not.

The phone rings, and it's Michael on the other end. "Good morning, Jaz! Did you sleep well?" He talks about his normal Saturday routine—the things he has planned for the day. The conversation is about life in general. Considering Michael has taken Jasmine to dinner on Wednesday and to a play on Friday, it is now time for her to see the fun side of him, where he rolls up his sleeves like a regular old guy.

The boys are having a get-together this Saturday, and he has already committed to be there. So to make sure that he keeps things rolling, he will extend an invitation to her. This is his chance to shine. He wants her to see his not-so-serious side, because there is nothing worse than a man who can't relax and enjoy himself. Pleased that she has accepted the invite to hang out with him and his friends, he asks her for permission to pick her up at her house around 6:00 p.m.

After the plans have been finalized, Jasmine glances at the clock. It's now about 10:30 a.m., and she already has a date for tonight. She's feeling pretty good about this man named Michael. She calls her girls to fill them in about the play and tell them that she is going with Michael to a barbeque at his friend's house.

Five o'clock rolls around and Jasmine is at home getting ready for Michael to pick her up. He arrives on time with a little box in hand. He hands her the box and asks that she not open it until she gets back home tonight. The excitement starts to build. She has a present that cannot be opened until she gets home—oh, the suspense! Jasmine thanks Michael for the gift and places the box on the bar so it will be the first thing she sees when she walks in tonight. While she is still in a daze about the box, Michael walks over and places his hand around her waist.

"Are you ready to go?"

"Uh, yes, I'm ready."

On the way over to the get together, Michael warns her about his friends and how they are always teasing him. Once there, he introduces her to everyone as his special friend. This is Michael's signal to his friends to start with the teasing. They begin to tease him about his past girlfriend and why he shouldn't let this new love interest go. During their Players' Club meeting, this is one of the tactics that they use to show the woman that she is special. Jasmine is feeling good because she thinks his boys seem to recognize that she's a real woman and Michael should listen to them.

Michael lets his playful side come out. He has shown her

the serious side with the business meeting at work, the wonderful dinner at the Italian restaurant, and front row seats at the play last night. Now he wants her to know that he is just a regular old guy and she can be relaxed and just be herself around him.

One of Michael's friends suggests a game of Spades. As Jasmine plays cards, her mind can't help but drift back to the box that is sitting on her bar. Even though she is enjoying the evening, if it ended in the next fifteen minutes, it would suit her fine. Michael glances over at Jasmine with a smile on his face because he notices that she is in deep thought; something or somebody has really captured her attention.

It's getting late, around 11:30 p.m., and she can't take the suspense any longer. The box has been on her mind all night and it has started to drive her crazy. Jasmine asks Michael if she can call it a night because she has to get up for church in the morning.

Michael says, "Sure, we can leave."

He tells his boys that he is leaving and will catch up with them tomorrow. He grabs Jasmine's hand and proceeds to walk to the door.

Michael asks, "What church do you attend?"

"I am a member at True Holiness."

"What time does church start?"

She hesitates for a moment before answering, "I usually go to the 11:00 a.m. service."

"Okay!" Michael says.

Arriving at Jasmine's house, Michael walks her to her door and thanks her for another wonderful evening. He wishes her a good night and says he will talk to her tomorrow. Jasmine says the feelings are mutual, but can't wait to close the door and see what is in that box. The first thing she does is kick off her shoes, then immediately she goes to the bar to retrieve the box. As she opens it slowly, excitement fills her body, and to her surprise it is Maxwell's "Now" CD. Her favorite—AHHH-HHHH! How sweet.

Just as Jasmine is about to pick up the phone to call Michael, she notices a piece of paper taped to the inside of the CD case. The note reads:

"Hello, Jaz, please listen to 'Lifetime.' I am dedicating this song to you. Sweet dreams, Love."

By this time, Jasmine is overwhelmed and rushes to pick up the phone to call Michael. Right away she thanks him for the CD.

"I hoped you would like it. I know how much you liked that CD, and I know you miss listening to it while you drive to work every morning. I wanted to bring a smile to your face. Jasmine, the pleasure was all mine. I know it's getting late and you have to get up for church in the morning, so I will talk to you tomorrow. Enjoy your CD."

"Thanks again, Michael. I will definitely enjoy my gift."

Jasmine hangs up the phone and pops the CD in. After hitting the repeat button several times, she snuggles in underneath the sheet as Maxwell's voice fills the room. She slowly drifts into a peaceful sleep.

Sunday morning arrives, and at 9:45 a.m. the alarm is going off. Michael reaches over to turn it off. Just as he's about to drift back into dreamland, he jumps up, "Jasmine!"

Michael normally spends Sunday morning catching up on sleep from the night before, but this Sunday is different. He realizes that he needs to keep things going so he can increase the chances of getting an invitation to Jasmine's house next week.

After a warm, wake-up shower, he calls her. The phone rings.

"Good morning, beautiful, this is Michael. Since we are having a guest speaker at my church today, I thought it would be okay to visit other churches. I was hoping to join you for service this morning."

"Sure," Jasmine stutters. "I'll meet you in front of the church around 10:45."

"Great," Michael says, "Oh! By the way, what colors are you wearing?"

Jasmine's not sure why he asks that, but she answers with, "I had planned on wearing a black dress."

"I thought I might wear a tie or something that would coordinate with the colors you are wearing. I need to go ahead and get dressed because it will take me a little longer to get there than you. I will meet you out front."

Jasmine now has to find her black dress. Even though she told Michael that was what she was wearing, in actuality she was just going to pin her hair up and throw on some slacks and a top.

Rambling through the closets, Jasmine comes across her black dress. She quickly throws it on and runs into the bathroom to bump a couple of curls in her hair. She glances at the clock and notices it is almost 10:30. She has told Michael she would meet him at 10:45, and it will take fifteen minutes to get there.

Michael arrives around 10:40 and stands in front of the church until Jasmine arrives. He has considered the possibility that she might be running late due to the fact this is a last minute hook-up.

Jasmine finally arrives and again asks Michael to forgive her tardiness. The church is packed and seating is limited. An usher signals to another usher standing with Jasmine and Michael that he has two seats available five rows from the front. The usher escorts them to their seats. Jasmine is hoping the lady over the Ladies Board is at church today because she is always asking her why she doesn't have a man in her life. This is Jasmine's opportunity to be seen with him. The usher asks Michael to fill out a visitor's card. The bishop finishes his sermon and it's announcement time. When it's Michael's turn to stand up and introduce himself, this tall, handsome man stands up and talks like he has been in church all his life. Michael says, "First, I would like to give thanks and glory unto God for allowing me to be here today. Also, thanks to the bishop and for a wonderful message. I am thoroughly enjoying myself and also would like to thank Jasmine for inviting me here today." He turns and looks at her briefly, "Thank you." Well put, Michael.

You see, Michael is a preacher's son. Need I say more? Jasmine sits in amazement! WOW! Okay, where did this guy come from? Not only is he thoughtful, caring, and smart, but most importantly, he is a God–fearing man, too.

Church service is over, and Michael invites Jasmine out to an early dinner. Lunch is the perfect time to set the stage. Jasmine has been a part of Michael's world for the past four days and this would be the perfect time to open up to her. Michael asks her to follow him to a nice, intimate seafood restaurant on the north side of town. At the restaurant, waiting to be seated, he tells her how comfortable he is around her and how he can't believe it's been only four days since the two of them met. He tells her that the past four days feel like weeks. But before he can go on, the hostess waves that their table is ready.

Michael has to be clever about his plan. If he can get Jasmine to feel like she has known him for a longer period of time, then she will be more open to sleeping with him by next week. He needs to make sure that after he and Jasmine are sexually close, she won't be calling him looking for a commitment instead of being the casual sexual partner he wants. His plan is to get her to believe that if she sticks it out with him that he will one day soon commit to a relationship with her. He accomplishes this task by giving her a number of legitimate excuses as to why he can't settle down right now. He also lets her know that he's open to a relationship, provided it's with the right woman. As the conversation continues during lunch, Michael brings up the question that he had asked her earlier that week.

"Jaz, do you remember when I asked you about your last relationship?"

"Yes, I do. Why, Michael?"

"Well, it has been a year since I have been in my last relationship. I didn't take enough time to get to know the last woman I was with. We kind of jumped into a relationship. Even though it lasted two years, one day she just left, no explanation, nothing. The last conversation she and I had was about marriage. She wanted to get married, and I wanted to wait until I was financially stable. I really don't think she understood my point of view.

"As I sit here and think about it, there were other problems as well. It was probably the best thing for both of us. In the two years we were together, I only remember her attending maybe two of my basketball games. She never liked to get involved in my activities like the basketball tournaments or getting together with the boys.

"Jaz, I want to be totally open with you. Communication is very important to me in a friendship."

Michael is putting it all on the table. He has to set this up just right so that later, after they are sexually active, he can refer back to this conversation and pull out key points that were made to her in the beginning. That way she can't say she didn't know.

Right now, as Jasmine listens to Michael speak about his personal experience, her thoughts are of his sincerity, his willingness to open up and share with her something that apparently is painful to him. Even though she is hearing him speak about not wanting to commit or being afraid to commit, she translates that to mean he is not at the point where he can place trust in her, but after she spends more time with him and they grow closer, he'll be ready to commit to her.

What Jasmine has to consider at this point is that Michael's time frame to settle down may be months or years away. She has to decide if the heartache that will come along is

MICHAEL IS PUTTING IT ALL ON THE TABLE. HE HAS TO SET THIS UP JUST RIGHT SO THAT LATER, AFTER THEY ARE SEXUALLY ACTIVE, HE CAN REFER BACK TO THIS CONVERSATION.

going to be worth it if Michael chooses someone other than herself.

Jasmine and Michael finish lunch. As they are about to leave the restaurant, Michael's cell phone rings. He asks if she would excuse him for a minute while he takes this call. It's his boys. He wants her to hear his conversation because he is now looking for a reason to end the day with her.

Michael answers his phone, "What's up, man! I'm having an early dinner with Jaz. Yeah, that's right. I'm with her again. Okay! We are finishing up here. I'll stop by in a minute."

"Jaz, I'm sorry. I have to go help one of the boys move. I promised him two weeks ago I would help him. I hope you don't count this against me."

"No, not at all. We'll talk later. Thanks for lunch."

Jasmine's phone rings about an hour after she gets home, and it's Michael.

"Hello, I just called to tell you I was thinking about you and I enjoyed church service this morning. Hopefully we can do it again sometime…Jaz, you're kind of quiet. Is everything okay?"

"Oh, yes. Everything is fine."

"Sweetie, me and the boys are almost finished moving. I am exhausted, and I should be home shortly. I'm going to rest for a minute and go to bed when I get home. I will call you from work in the morning."

The moment of truth is upon Michael to see if his hard work will pay off. He calls Jaz Monday morning like he has been doing for the past two days to stay consistent.

"Morning, baby."

"Hi, Michael." Jasmine smiles though the phone.

"I was wondering if you wanted to stop by my place after work."

"Sure, love to. Call me later with directions?"

"No problem. See you then," Michael says.

Later that evening, Michael's doorbell rings. He pauses, hand on the knob, waiting for a second ring or knock. The doorbell rings again. He opens the door with a wide smile on his face. Jaz walks in wearing jeans and a nice fitting top. A little puzzled, Michael asks, "Is that what you wore to work?"

"Of course not," says Jaz, "I ran by the house so I could freshen up a little."

Jaz compliments Michael on how well he keeps his place. She stands for a minute looking around. Michael asks her if she would care for something to drink.

"Can I have some water, please?"

"Sure."

Not sure if she wants the water ice cold or not, he brings her a glass with some ice cubes and a warm bottle of water.

As the time passes and the water trickles through her body, she asks if she can use the bathroom. Michael points her in the right direction. He uses this moment to light a few candles, turn down the lights a bit, and grab a breath strip. After about three minutes, Jaz returns with a smile on her face. She wasn't expecting his bathroom to be as clean and well-decorated as it was. She is feeling good and pretty comfortable at this point.

By spending so much time with him the last four days, Jaz feels at ease with Michael, so she is open to a little cuddling and kissing. As far as she is concerned, Michael is the perfect gentleman. He is a man she considers dating and investing time in, so she decides to go ahead and become intimate with him.

After falling asleep in Michael's strong arms, she awakes in his bed and realizes what time it is and decides she needs to go so she can get to work on time. Once Michael sees her out the door, the celebration starts. His plan worked.

Two months later, everything is going fine by Michael's definition. They have been talking and seeing each other regularly. Michael calls her at work like he has been doing for the past two months.

"Hi, Jaz! Are you working hard or hardly working?" he jokes. "I am going over to Terry's house after work, and I have a couple of errands to run, but I will call you when I am on my way over. Okay?"

"Sure!" Jaz replies.

This would be a good time to catch up with the girls. They decide to head back to Visions, grab a bite to eat and listen to some jazz for a little while.

They pick a table close to the stage where the jazz band is playing so Jasmine's girlfriend, Linda, can keep an attentive eye on prospective single men in the club. They are proceeding to order, when Linda looks over Jasmine's

BY SPENDING SO MUCH TIME WITH HIM THE LAST FOUR DAYS, JAZ FEELS AT EASE WITH MICHAEL, SO SHE IS OPEN TO A LITTLE CUDDLING AND KISSING.

shoulder to see Michael walking in with another woman. She hesitates and then says, "Um, Jaz, isn't that Michael over there?"

"Where?"

"At the door, looking around," Linda says.

As Jasmine turns to see for herself, she is overwhelmed with rage. But considering her girls are there, she has to play it cool. "You're right, Linda. That is Michael. Maybe I will go and speak." Jasmine gets up from her table and walks over to the front of the club to speak to him, but then decides just to let it go for now.

When Jaz returns to the table, her girls ask if she wants to leave and, of course, she does. In this situation, what woman wants to sit there with her girls and watch the man she has spent almost every day of the last few months with wine and dine another woman?

Even though she was a perfect lady in front of the girls, inside she is brokenhearted. She can't wait to get home. Michael has a lot of explaining to do. He calls twenty minutes after Jaz gets home to let her know he is on his way.

"Hey, Jaz, I'm on my way over there, but I wanted to see if you wanted me to bring you something."

"No, I'm fine, baby, the sooner you get here the better. Besides, the girls and I stopped by Visions for a bite to eat earlier."

Michael, not knowing what to say at this point, makes an excuse that his cell phone battery is low and he will see her in a few minutes. He needs this time to think of something just in case Jaz saw him and the other woman. Michael arrives and greets her with a hug and kiss. But before he can get comfortable, she hits him with the question. "Michael, is there anything you want to tell me?"

"No, babe, except I missed you today."

"Really, now. Was that before or after you were at Visions? I was at Visions tonight and saw you with another woman. I thought we were together."

Sounding surprised, Michael replies, "You were at Visions? I didn't see you there."

"But I saw you. You and that woman! Michael, I repeat, is there something you need to tell me?"

"No, Jaz, honey. Why didn't you come over and speak to me?"

Just as these words slither from Michael's lips, Jasmine looks up at him with this blank look in her eyes. He can clearly see that she is confused and hurt. Michael stops for a minute to gather his thoughts, before saying anything else.

"Jaz, you know I like spending time with you and we have a lot of fun together, but like I told you in the beginning, I want to take my time and really get to know the next woman I settle down with. I said I wasn't ready right now, but I do enjoy the quality time I spend with you."

Michael, remembering the conversation they had after church that one afternoon, quickly makes reference to the things that they talked about.

"Jaz, the last thing I want to do is get hurt or to hurt some-one I care about, and I do care about you. Yes, I went to grab a bite to eat with a friend. But that's all it was—a bite to eat. Jaz, I have brought you into my world, around my friends and everything else. I just need time, baby. That's all I'm asking for—just a little more time before I jump into this commitment thing."

"Michael, if you can't make a commitment to me, then, I guess we won't be seeing each other anymore."

"Jaz! Jaz! I didn't say I wouldn't commit to you. I just need a little more time, you know. I just want to make sure you are the right one!"

"Michael, you need to leave."

"Jaz!"

"Michael, just go."

"Okay."

Michael leaves, but he knows everything is all right. You see, Jaz just needs a little time to think, to be alone with her feelings. She goes into the kitchen, pours herself a glass of wine and takes a seat on the staircase. She replays the last two months over and over in her head to see where she made her mistake in thinking that she and Michael were in a relationship. She remembers all the nice things he has done for her like replacing her favorite CD she lost, the picnic, morning calls and other little things.

She thinks about the conversation they had after church that one afternoon and the fact that Michael did continuously tell her he was not ready to commit. But he was willing to talk about his life and volunteered personal information. He never referred to her as his girlfriend, but as a friend or special lady friend, and she never did actually hear Michael say, "It's a date." He would say, "We could go hang out," or something general like that.

AS SHE SITS THERE, SHE REALIZES THAT THE SIGNS WERE THERE IN THE BEGINNING, BUT SHE IGNORED THEM. JASMINE LEANS BACK ON THE STAIRCASE AND MUMBLES TO HERSELF.

"Damn," Jaz says out loud.

As she sits there, she realizes that the signs were there in the beginning, but she ignored them. Jasmine leans back on the staircase and mumbles to herself.

"Well, Jaz, you did it again. I guess it's my fault because I assumed, and I didn't ask Michael what type of relationship we had. I thought we were together. In all actuality, Michael can see anyone he wants to."

After a long, sleepless night, she decides to call Michael at work the next day to tell him that she is still willing to see him. It's hard to let go now and Michael knows it, because she is emotionally attached to him. Michael beats her to it by calling her first at work.

"Hey, girl!"

"Hi, I—"

"Hold on, me first."

Jasmine pauses in mid-sentence to let Michael speak.

"I wanted to apologize for last night, but I just need some more time to make sure you are the one for me. I care about you, and I still want to see you."

Michael wants to end the conversation over the phone

HE KNOWS IF SHE LETS HIM COME OVER OR SHE COMES OVER TO HIS HOUSE, HE CAN DO A BETTER JOB OF PLEADING HIS CASE.

as quickly as possible and talk about it in person tonight over the flicker of candles burning. He knows if she lets him come over or she comes over to his house, he can do a better job of pleading his case. Jasmine agrees to his coming over, but she has already made up her mind that she still wants to see him.

Later at Jasmine's house, Michael is hoping to make up and have a passionate night of sex. He knows she enjoys having sex with him. He knows he has to put in extra work tonight to keep this casual sexual relationship going. At this point, he begins to play on the weakness a woman has for a man— the "Trump Card."

9

CHAPTER NINE
SKILL LEVEL III:
MR. COMPLETE

Let's look at the men who have moved to yet another level of the game and are masters of the craft. These men are calculating and, at the same time, very smooth. They typify characters like those in Hollywood-produced movies. These men compliment women like they breathe air. Even though these men are similar to the Derricks and the Michaels of the world, there is one element that places them in a class of their own. So pay attention.

When conversing with them, you will feel like the world revolves around you, and, like Michael, these men will have you thinking their only reason for waking up in the morning is to spend time with you. But you have to pay close attention to how these men are using their words and the way their actions affect you and others around you. The best description for these types of men is DANGEROUS. Dangerous indeed. After reading about Michael, it is easy to understand how a woman might want to cry. But after dealing with this next type of man, she might want to hurt somebody.

BUT AFTER DEALING WITH THIS NEXT TYPE OF MAN, SHE MIGHT WANT TO HURT SOMEBODY.

Men on this level have realized that words alone and actions alone are not enough. They understand that to get to the cream of the crop, they must practice what they preach. That's right, their words and actions must be in tune.

What I mean by the cream of the crop are intelligent women who are serious about dating only men who are looking for marriage. These women have learned from their mistakes and have listened and taken the advice of their male friends. They have lost a few battles along the way but still manage to pull themselves back together and love again.

Men know if they are going to be successful in these chess matches, they must step up their game. Ambitious students of the arts, they seek out new information on love and relationships daily. These types of men will expose their feelings very early by bringing up a conversation about relationships and marriage. They want to lead the woman to believe they are sincere, a man ready to be the provider, the king of a castle with a beautiful queen by his side. And even though they may be telling the truth concerning what they want down the road, you have to look out for the words they use in the mean time.

They know that they have to lead the woman to feel that the two of them are looking for the same thing without exact-

THESE TYPES OF MEN WILL EXPOSE THEIR FEELINGS VERY EARLY BY BRINGING UP A CONVERSATION ABOUT RELATIONSHIPS AND MARRIAGE. THEY WANT TO LEAD THE WOMAN TO BELIEVE THEY ARE SINCERE, A MAN READY TO BE THE PROVIDER, THE KING OF A CASTLE WITH A BEAUTIFUL QUEEN BY HIS SIDE.

ly saying it. Excuses such as: "I've been hurt before," "I am working on my career," and "You know you are my Boo" will not work anymore. These men have moved on to other techniques that would suggest that they are looking for the same thing that she is looking for. "I am ready to settle down," "I am ready to get married," and "I am just waiting for that one real woman to walk into my life." They have to elevate their actions past the movies, dinner, plays, and on to other things. Like outings in the park where the sunset shadows her face as it sets

EVEN THOUGH THIS MAN HAS DONE HER WRONG, FOR SOME REASON SHE FEELS IF SHE STAYS IN TOUCH THAT SHE WILL SOMEHOW MAKE A DIFFERENCE IN THIS MAN'S LIFE. SHE BELIEVES THAT HE WILL STOP AND THINK TO HIMSELF THAT THIS WOMAN REALLY CARES ENOUGH TO STAY AROUND AFTER ALL THE BAD THINGS HE HAS DONE AND IS CONCERNED ENOUGH TO CALL HIM AND CHECK ON HIM.

behind the horizon of the lake, or a trip to his momma's house solely to introduce his new love to her. And of course a visit to the jeweler to size her finger and look at rings that would be symbolic of his love for her.

A woman might run into a man that she just cannot get out of her mind no matter how hard she tries and no matter how many so-called relationships she enters in and out of. There is a little voice in the back of her head that holds on to the fact that someday he will change and be with only her. There is nothing a woman can do to change a man's mind, but to hold on to that hope, she calls him a couple of times a month just to see how he is doing, maybe talk for a minute to catch up on what's going on in his world. Even though this man has done her wrong, for some reason she feels if she stays in touch that she will somehow make a difference in this man's life. She believes that he will stop and think to himself that this woman really cares enough to stay around after all the bad things he has done and is concerned enough to call him and check on him.

Reality check—men at this level have ongoing sexual relationships with women dating back four, five or six plus years before. They have a steady rotation of women, old and new. They could care less about the phone calls or the concern a woman is trying to show them. They have done what they have set out to do and that was to keep her in a false relation-ship with the intent of fair exchange.

When she is surrounded by the quietness of her own thoughts, she might want to ask herself this question. Why does this one man stand out from the rest? This man has sepa-rated himself so far apart from the rest of the men in her life that she can't stop thinking about him for a long period of time.

97

THIS MAN HAS SEPARATED HIMSELF SO FAR APART FROM THE REST OF THE MEN IN HER LIFE THAT SHE CAN'T STOP THINKING ABOUT HIM FOR A LONG PERIOD OF TIME. IT'S THE THINGS HE DOES FOR HER AND HOW HE MAKES HER FEEL. IT'S THE WORDS HE USES AND HOW THEY MAKE HER FEEL. IT'S THE UNSELFISHNESS, THE WILLINGNESS TO PLEASE HER IN THE BEDROOM. HE WOULD GIVE UP OR POSTPONE HIS OWN SEXUAL GRATIFICATION IN ORDER TO PLEASE HER TOTALLY, BUT ONE THING HE WILL NOT DO IS TELL HER HE LOVES HER.

It's the things he does for her and how he makes her feel. It's the words he uses and how they make her feel. It's the unselfishness, the willingness to please her in the bedroom. He would give up or postpone his own sexual gratification in order to please her totally, but one thing he will not do is tell her he loves her.

THEY HAVE FIGURED OUT A WAY TO GET WOMEN TO SLEEP WITH THEM WITHOUT SAYING, "I LOVE YOU."

If women were to ask these Level III men if they loved them during the midst of sex, more than likely they would find a way around the question. They have figured out a way to get women to sleep with them without saying, "I love you." This will cut down on their cars being scratched up, windows being broken out, or getting embarrassed in public when they are out with other women.

How do men accomplish this? They use words to suggest that they love her and want to be with her without telling her directly. I believe women make the mistake of replacing the words he uses with the words *you, me, and us,* instead of listening to what the man is really saying. I feel women only hear what they want to hear and not what they should hear.

To clarify my statement, consider this. When speaking with these particular men, a woman may hear a comment such as, "I am looking for a long-lasting relationship where I have her back and she has mine, a healthy relationship that eventually will lead to marriage." She might translate these words to mean he is looking for a long-lasting relationship where the two of *us* can grow together to become one, where I got *your* back and *you* got mine, a healthy relationship that leads to marriage with *me*.

This is a perfect example of how she hears what she wants to hear and not what is said. Not at any time in those male-spoken words did he use *us, you* or *me*. So always ponder this question: When speaking of relationships, is he referring to you or is he speaking generally? Don't be afraid to ask direct questions. His answers will either incorporate you into this life plan, or his answers will continue to speak in a general tone.

A MAN GENERALLY KNOWS WHEN HE FIRST MEETS A WOMAN WHAT CATEGORY SHE FALLS INTO. SHE WILL EITHER BE PLACED INTO THE WIFE POOL OR INTO THE BOOTY CALL CLASSIFICATION.

A man generally knows when he first meets a woman what category she falls into. She will either be placed into the wife pool or into the booty call classification. If she is placed in the wife's pool, she will be treated with more respect. He soon will begin to share more of his things freely and look for ways to make her life easier. In the booty call classification, she gets treated with respect to a limited degree. He will only do the bare minimum to keep her around and content with the relationship.

That's why the first two-week period is very important. This time will determine if she stays in that particular category or not. In the majority of cases, it doesn't take a man six months or a year to decide if she is the one for him. He is often looking for inconsistencies throughout the dating process to eliminate her. A woman should make sure she gets a definite confirmation about the direction her relationship is heading in. She shouldn't give him an ultimatum or pressure him into a commitment, but establish a time frame that works for her and stick to it. She shouldn't let him know what her time frame is because he will use that information to keep her in the relationship with a false hope. But beware. There are consequences for the choices you make, whether the choice is a good one or bad one. Make sure you are willing to deal with the repercussions that come with your decision before you make a move. You can even checkmate yourself trying to checkmate someone else.

10

CHAPTER TEN
DEVON MCNEIL

"I will be sleeping with someone's daughter before the end of this conference. She just doesn't know it yet." – Devon

It is the first day of registration for the 10th Annual CPA Conference. Devon enters through the rotating glass doors of the hotel. He loves to attend these types of conferences because there are a few women from out of town and he knows he can talk one or two of them into making this a sex-filled weekend. Walking through the luxurious five-star hotel foyer, he smiles at the two ladies working at the front desk as he passes by. Not knowing where he is going, he decides to walk over to the front desk to ask for directions, at least that's what he wants the ladies to think. He is really checking out the possibilities of one of them fulfilling his weekend quest.

After getting directions, he heads towards the conference area. Walking up to take his place in line, a woman sits in the middle chair behind the registration table. Her attractive, full lips, baby-doll smile, and seductive, cat-like eyes catch his attention. He wishes she were standing up so he could see her full body. He would hate to get all excited and then be disappointed when she stood up.

The registration line is long. With his mind full of anticipation, his first thought is to skip, but instead, he relaxes and takes his rightful place in line. The line is moving quickly. He decides to calculate his position in order to make the most of this opportunity.

With one person left standing in front of him now, the call for the next person in line comes from the lady to the far right. He has timed it perfectly. At that moment, one simple word will take on a totally different meaning. "Next," the lady seated in the middle says. He is now standing in front of her.

"Hello, sir. May I have your name?" She speaks in a soft but authoritative voice.

"Oh, um, Devon, Devon McNeil."

When she gets up, his wish is granted. She goes to skim through the late registration packets looking for Mr. McNeil's name because she doesn't see him on the list.

"Oh, baby," he says to himself. The curve of her hips is exactly what he has hoped for.

"Okay. Here you go, Mr. McNeil," she says as she turns back to give Devon his packet and ID badge.

"The first meeting will start at one o'clock in the Imperial Ballroom. Enjoy the conference."

"Thank you," Devon says. Before he can ask her for her name, she has already called for the next person in line. So he turns and walks away.

Thinking to himself that this is going to be a good weekend, he lightly tosses his keys up in the air and nods his head, signaling that he has a job to do.

At this point, Devon has found two possible women to fulfill his quest for the weekend, but like most players in the game, they never choose early. They always want to see all of their options before making a selection. It's like shopping in the produce aisle

AT THIS POINT, DEVON HAS FOUND TWO POSSIBLE WOMEN TO FULFILL HIS QUEST FOR THE WEEKEND, BUT LIKE MOST PLAYERS IN THE GAME, THEY NEVER CHOOSE EARLY. THEY ALWAYS WANT TO SEE ALL OF THEIR OPTIONS BEFORE MAKING A SELECTION.

of the grocery store, looking through a basket of peaches hoping to find that one ripe peach that will taste so sweet.

He looks at his watch to see how much time he has until the first meeting starts. With a couple hours to spare and the anticipation of a productive weekend, Devon decides to check into the hotel.

One of the ladies he has met earlier at the front desk greets him with a warm smile and a friendly, "Hello. How can I help you?" He can tell she is interested by the way her eyes look up at him. He responds by asking her if they have any available rooms for the weekend. Taking a minute to search through the hotel's computer system, she finds some vacancies that will accommodate him.

"Yes, we have some rooms available. The first one is on the second floor, and it comes with two full-size beds."

"No, I can't do the full-size beds. Plus, I might need room for someone else," he says very seductively.

"You do seem a bit tall for the full-size beds," she responds, letting out a slight giggle. "Okay. There is a queen-size bed on the first floor, but it is a smoking room."

With a smirk on his face, he thinks to himself, *This is going to be too easy.*

"We are getting close with the beds, but I would prefer a nonsmoking room. Do you have a room anywhere that's non-smoking with a king-size bed?"

"Let me see. It looks like there is one on the 12th floor in the west wing of the hotel. Would that work for you?"

"That would be great."

"I will need to see your driver's license, and will you be

paying by credit card?"

"Okay. Here is my driver's license, and I hope you accept American Express."

"We sure do, Mr. McNeil," she says, looking at his driver's license.

A couple of minutes later, she gives him the key to room 1202 and instructs him on how to get there.

"By the way, can you have the bellman bring my bags up to my room, unless you…want to bring them up later personally?"

"No, I can't do that," she says, slightly embarrassed. "But I will have the bellman bring your bags up to your room."

"Okay," he says, looking at her smiling. "My bags are in the trunk of my car. I am parked right out front. Here is my valet ticket, and have him leave the ticket on the night stand for me, please."

"That will not be a problem, Mr. McNeil."

"Thank you so much."

As Devon is on his way to the find his room in the west wing of the hotel, he is stopped by an old man who seems very intrigued with him.

"Excuse me, sir. You look like the type of man who likes a good pair of shoes and likes to keep them shined. May I shine your shoes for you?"

The old man's stubby gray beard and dingy white shirt catches Devon off guard, but he quickly remembers rule number three of the player's handbook. A quality woman always checks a man's shoes out, and he doesn't want to be caught slipping. He steps up onto the platform, places his briefcase down beside him, eases his way into the chair, and places both of his black square-toe shoes on the shoe stands.

Noticing the uniqueness and quality of the craftsmanship of his shoes, the old man asks Devon where he bought his shoes.

"I have been shining shoes here, let me see, about twenty years now, and I have found out that you can tell a lot about a man from the type of shoes he wears. Let me guess. You are a doctor."

"No."

"Lawyer."

"No."

"I know. You're here from out of town for the CPC, no CPD conference. You know, one of those people who works with numbers."

"Yeah! I am here for the CPA's Conference this weekend, but I am not here from out of town. I live here."

"I have been seeing a lot of fine women here today."

"I know what you mean," Devon smiles, leaning down to slap the old man's hand.

With four or five brush strokes and snaps of the polishing towel, one of Devon's shoes has the luster of a flawless diamond. "Man, you are good," Devon says, looking down at his shoe.

Pleased with the results, he settles back in his chair. He

takes out the conference agenda to see what they have planned for them this weekend. He is happy to see there is a party this evening hosted by the local radio station in the Majestic Ballroom following the network mixer. He figures this will be the perfect setting for him to meet some quality women, or better yet, some potential opponents. He takes out his cell phone and calls his best friend, Steve, to tell him about the women he has seen and the party tonight.

"Yo, this Steve."

"Hey, Steve. Man, the women down here at the hotel are fine."

"For real."

"Yeah, I have already found one that is a definite for tonight. The radio station that you like is hosting a party here this evening, so you don't want to be left out."

"Okay. I will be there."

Snap...Snap...The trademark sound of a skilled shoeshine man's towel putting on the finishing shine interrupts his conversation with Steve.

In a slow raspy voice the old man says, "They look as good as new."

Devon can't help but agree. Ending his call with Steve, he asks the old man if he can shine two other pairs of shoes he brought with him. Having agreed to shine his shoes, Devon gives the man forty dollars and tells him to keep the change.

Devon asks if the old man will have the concierge bring them to his room once he's finished.

The old man says, "Sure, and remember to get a fine honey for me."

They both laugh, and Devon heads to his room to get his shoes before the first workshop. On the elevator, he thinks about the body of the woman behind the registration desk and hopes she will still be there when he comes back.

After dropping off his shoes, he returns to the place where he signed in. The registration desk is packed up. He shrugs his shoulders and thinks to himself, *Oh well. Maybe I will see her later on this weekend.*

Before he finishes his thought, he hears someone call his name. "Hello, Mr. McNeil," the lady from the front desk says, passing by.

"Hi," Devon says when he turns around to see who has called him. Pausing for a second, he thinks to himself, *Hmm, I don't know. This is a little too easy.*

He makes his way to the first workshop. After the five-hour workshop, Devon looks at his watch. Dinnertime! He figures he'll retire to his room, order room service, unwind from a long day, and possibly take a nap before the mixer and party later.

Once in his room, he sets the alarm clock for 7:00 p.m. He calls downstairs for a house salad and blackened catfish served over rice. Room service says it will be about thirty or forty minutes. Devon decides to take advantage of this time before dinner by taking a shower.

He opens the shower's glass door, twists the brass knob to

the left, setting the water to a soothing warm temperature. The force from the tiny water drops massages his body all over. "Mmm," he says. "That feels good."

Feeling relaxed from the shower, Devon turns the water off. Before he gets out to dry himself off, he hears the room door close. He opens the glass door, and says, "Hello?" He wraps a towel around himself before walking out of the bathroom.

Seeing the tray on the dresser, he figures it must have been room service. Devon can smell the food's aroma coming from underneath the tray's top. When he lifts it, the food looks good. With the last bite of fish completing a full stomach and a warm shower, he doesn't have a problem drifting off for a nap.

At 7:00 p.m., the alarm clock sounds. Devon stretches his arms and eases out of bed. Thinking about what he is going to wear tonight, he retrieves his garment bag from the closet and lays out his black suit along with a pressed French Cufflinks black shirt with bold white strips. He places both pairs of shoes on the bed to see which one he might wear with this arrangement. While trying to decide, he breaks the plastic lock on the mini-bar and fixes himself a glass of Remy Martin V.S.O.P. with a splash of OJ. Shortly after finishing off his drink and slipping into his attire for the evening, he looks at himself in the mirror and thinks, *Yeah, this outfit is going to work. It gives me that sophisticated look but has a jovial feel.* He grabs his cell phone and heads downstairs for the mixer.

When he arrives, he looks around to see who or where he might start tonight, not wanting to make a player mistake by choosing early. He spots his friend Steve talking with a group of guys and decides to make his way over to them. They are in the midst of a heated conversation about which NBA division, East or West, has the best teams.

Steve sees Devon approaching them and wants to ask Devon for his opinion. "I am glad Devon's showed up so he can shed some light on this for you all. Hey, Devon, you played ball in college, right?"

"Yeah. Why? What's up?"

"Would you tell these guys that the Western conference teams in the NBA are stronger than the Eastern conference teams?"

"Steve, you know I love Philly, but I am going to have to give the edge to the West…But I am sorry guys. Why are we here talking about basketball? What we should be doing is getting to know some of these women in here. With that being said, let's head to the bar, and this round of drinks is on me." Devon's eyes prowl the room like a big cat looking for its prey.

As Devon turns, he bumps into a woman passing by. "Excuse me! Let me get a napkin for you. I am sorry. I wasn't looking. I didn't even see you coming."

"No problem. That's okay."

Devon looks at her very puzzled for a moment.

"Hold up! Wait a minute. You are the lady from the registration desk this morning. My apologies again for the mishap." This could not have worked out any more perfectly. Now, Devon does not feel badly at all about spilling his drink on her.

"That's okay," she smiles and dabs at a spot on her suit jacket. Devon pauses, as if searching for a topic.

"I didn't catch your name this morning, and I believe it's only fair since you know mine."

"Is that your way of asking for my name?"

"Okay. Let's start over. Hello, my name is Devon, Devon McNeil, and yours might be?"

"It's Tonya Williams."

"Nice to meet you, Tonya. Are you in town for the conference?"

"No, I live here."

"Would it be safe to assume you work in the accounting field?"

"I am a Finance Manager for Nation One Motor Credit."

"Very impressive," Devon says.

"Do you work in the industry as well?"

"I have been in this industry for ten years. I am now the VP of Business Development for PSK Consulting."

"Do you have a business card by any chance?"

"Sure." As Devon turns to set his glass down to provide one of his business cards for Tonya, he glances toward the ballroom's entrance.

There stands a tall, elegant woman wearing a black, strapless dress looking a bit lost or confused. He thinks to himself,

I wonder who she is looking for, or better yet, did she come by herself. Devon is with what he thinks was the sweetest peach, but after glancing around the room, now he thinks that he may have seen a peach that is even sweeter.

He does not want to be caught staring at this woman, so he collects himself and tries to focus his attention on Tonya.

Although he wants to find out more about Tonya, he can't help being drawn to this other woman. Watching as she walks through the crowd as if there was a dedicated light following her every move, and wanting desperately to know if she came by herself, he positions himself to catch a glimpse of her.

Unaware of Devon's lack of attention, Tonya continues talking, but the allure of the woman's beauty is too much for him to ignore. He politely excuses himself from Tonya. He tells her that he needs to talk with a client that has just walked in.

Devon doesn't want to approach the elegant woman just yet, so he figures that if he engages in small talk with a client, he can eventually make his way over to the elegant woman when he is sure that Tonya is not watching. So he stops by to visit with Jim Brown, the CFO for Chambers Studios, who is far enough away from Tonya but still in eyesight of the mystery woman.

He congratulates Mr. Brown on how well Chambers Studios has done this past month and wishes them much success in the coming months.

"Thank you," Jim replies. He goes on to say, "Your company has done a great job for us, and I know this might not be the most opportune time, but I am sad to say that we have decided to bring the accounting responsibilities in-house. Since we are all here, I would like for you to meet my new Director of Financial Accounting and Reporting who will be heading the accounting department. Vanessa," Jim calls, signaling her with his hand to come over. "Vanessa Lewis, I would like you to meet Devon McNeil. Devon's company has been doing our financial reporting for the past three years. You two should set up a meeting to discuss the transition back in-house."

This cannot be happening to me, Devon thinks to himself. *My company's biggest client is leaving, and the woman I've been looking at all night is heading their new accounting department. NO! NO! Settle down, Devon, remain calm.*

"Vanessa, congratulations on your new position with Chambers Studios. I know you will like it there. The management team is great, and the company is very stable."

"Thank you, Devon."

"Well, Vanessa, when would you like to schedule a meeting to discuss the transition?" Devon asks.

Vanessa replies, "I will call your office on Monday to make the official announcement, and then we can discuss our plans to bring the accounting in-house."

"Okay...Vanessa, I don't remember seeing your face around town at any of the local CPA events. Are you from this area?" Devon asks.

"No. I just moved from Atlanta to take this position about

a month ago."

Knowing if Vanessa lives locally will determine what Devon's next move will be. If she lives in the area, then he will opt to take a more subtle approach instead of aggressively pursuing a sexual encounter for the weekend. So while he's shocked by the professional blow he's just taken, Devon is not deterred from pursuing his other objectives.

"Oh, I see. How do you like it so far?"

"I like it here, but I miss my family and friends. Not to mention Princess, my one-year-old Maltese. I had to leave her behind for now."

"I'm sorry to hear that. Sounds like you are very fond of her. It must of have been a hard decision to leave everything behind to come here."

"Sometimes in life you have to make those hard decisions in order reach the goals you have planned for yourself."

Sensing a disconnection between them and wanting a moment to gather his thoughts, he asks if she would like another glass of wine.

"Vanessa, I could use another drink. Would you like another glass of wine?" Devon says.

"Sure. I would like that. A glass of Merlot, please."

"Okay."

As the bartender finishes mixing his drink, Steve taps him on his shoulder.

"Devon, what's up man? Who is the honey you were talking to a minute ago?"

"Steve, you won't believe the night I am having. That alluring woman you saw me talking to is the new Director of Financial Accounting and Reporting, and guess for who."

"Who?"

"Chambers Studios."

"That's good! That means you will get a chance to see her again."

"No, man, you don't understand. They're bringing their accounting in-house.

"Ohoo!"

"Yeah! I know."

"Well, good luck with that."

"Steve, I will catch up with you later. I have to take her drink to her. Bartender, put it on my tab."

He returns with a glass of merlot for Vanessa.

"Thank you," she says. "So, Devon, how long have you been in the accounting field?"

"Um, about ten...."

Then looking down, Vanessa stops Devon in mid-sentence to excuse herself when she feels the vibration of her cell phone in her purse. "I don't mean to cut you off, but I just saw a couple of people I need to talk with. I'll be in touch with you on Monday," she says, before walking away.

After Vanessa abruptly ends their conversation, Devon walks away shaking his head and smiling. He saw her cell phone's green light blinking in her purse. When he makes it over to Steve and the other guys, they are still debating about the NBA. Before Devon can be drawn into the discussion, Tonya sees him walking alone and makes her way back over.

"Hi, Devon. Are you enjoying yourself?" she asks.

"Sure," he answers, but his mind is on winning some brownie points with Vanessa and just brainstorming ways he can get closer to her.

Aware of Tonya's interest, he continues to fuel her ideas of him being a potential husband. He talks about his outlook on life and how this special person would play an essential part in his life. He wants to paint the picture that he could be the man that Tonya has been looking for all of her life. But it is all just part of his plan to win Tonya's affection. He is hoping she will hear what he's saying and see herself being a part of his life.

With hopes of one last conversation with Vanessa before the end of the night, the small talk with Tonya soon grows tiresome, but this time Devon does not have to excuse himself. Her needing to visit the ladies' room draws her away.

Devon notices Vanessa leaving, so he follows her into the hallway. Uncertain about the impression he has made on her, he does not want to wait until Monday to speak with her again.

"Vanessa, wait! I am glad I was able to catch you before you left. I remembered looking over the schedule and noticing that there is some free time tomorrow after lunch. I was hoping we could have lunch and talk about the transitional phase. I have some ideas that will help make the transition flow smoothly."

Vanessa, not seeming too interested in meeting with him

tomorrow, offers her apologies and tells him that she will have her assistant call him and set up a meeting for next week.

He is not going to let her get away that easily, but for now he wishes her a good night and hopes she enjoys the rest of the conference.

When Devon returns to the party, Steve tells him that Tonya came by looking for him a minute ago. At this point, he isn't feeling up to chatting with Tonya, or the guys, for that matter. Devon finishes his last drink and calls it a night.

The next morning, Devon awakes from a sleepless night with thoughts of Vanessa on his mind. He thinks about the way she has brushed him off. *She must not know who I am. I am Devon McNeil. It's obvious she doesn't know my motto. I am every woman's dream and every man's worst nightmare. But that's okay. I'll be ready for her next week.*

After two scrambled eggs, toast, and a glass of orange juice, Devon walks into the morning workshop room looking for a place to sit. He sees Tonya sitting alone waiting for the workshop to start.

"Hey, are you saving this seat for me?" Devon asks with a smile.

"Of course I am," Tonya replies.

As the meeting begins, Tonya and Devon open their briefcases and remove pens and legal pads, preparing to take notes. By late afternoon, they are making faces at one another, not paying attention at all, and passing notes back and forth.

Devon passes the first note. On it he has written, "Will

you go out with me? Circle 'Yes' or 'No' or 'Maybe.' " Tonya replies by marking "Maybe." They laugh, trying not to make too much noise.

Devon decides to try again. This time the note reads, "Do you want to ditch the rest of the meeting and go grab a bite to eat? Check 'Yes' or 'No.' "

Tonya opens the note and giggles. She is amused that he has eliminated the "Maybe" box. She checks the "Yes" box, and then passes the folded paper back to him.

Devon writes a final message asking if she would like to get something to eat outside of the hotel and to meet him at the front of the hotel in five minutes. Agreeing to the plan, Tonya places her legal pad back into her briefcase and walks out of the room.

Five minutes later, Devon leaves the ballroom, stopping by his room to pick up his valet ticket. When he opens the door, he notices the red light blinking on the phone. He picks up the handset to listen to his message.

"Hi, Mr. McNeil. This is Michelle from the front desk. I hope you don't mind me calling you in your room. If you don't get in too late tonight, feel free to give me a call at ###-###-####. Talk to you later." Devon wasn't expecting this message and pats his pockets searching for his phone to capture Michelle's number.

Down in the lobby, Tonya stands patiently waiting for Devon before walking over to the front desk and asking for a couple of extra towels to be sent to her room. The bell sounds, the doors open, and out walks Devon from the elevator.

When Devon approaches the front desk, Michelle's face brightens. Tonya observes the difference in Michelle's demeanor when Devon places his hand around her waist and asks if she is ready to go.

He reaches into his jacket pocket to get his ticket to give to the valet attendant, but not before winking at Michelle as they turn to walk away.

In the car, Devon asks Tonya what she would like to eat. She has a taste for some fajitas. So Devon takes her to a great place not too far from the hotel that serves the best Mexican cuisine.

Inside the restaurant, after being seated, Devon asks if she has eaten there before. Since Tonya isn't familiar with the restaurant, Devon suggests they go with the party platter. The fajitas, enchiladas, nachos, and quesadillas would offer a variety. Devon orders the house special margarita for them both, and as they sit for a while just getting to know each other, laughter and chatter hover over their table.

The warm setting sun's rays shine through the restaurant's window, and the swaying tree branches plant a thought in Devon's mind.

"Tonya, I have an idea. Do you have time?"

"Yeah, what do you have in mind?" Tonya replies with a tone of curiosity and confusion.

"Go ahead and finish your drink. There is something special I want to show you."

"Okay."

Devon stumbled across a secluded lake on the outskirts of town one evening when he got lost heading home from his weekend retreat cabin in the mountains. He remembered how beautiful the lake looked with the sun setting just behind it.

As Tonya finishes her last margarita, Devon gestures to the waiter for the check. After leaving the restaurant and once inside of Devon's car, Tonya pins her hair back to keep it from blowing in her face. They are heading Northbound out of town on the main interstate highway when Devon lowers the volume on the car stereo and says, "You know, Tonya, when I just want to get away and put life's struggles behind me, I let the top down, stop by my favorite quiet spot, and let Kenny G's soothing saxophone take me to a place far, far away. Do you know what I mean?"

"Yeah, I know what you mean. I have my little thing I do as well to escape from the demands that life puts on me."

As Tonya is finishing her thought and fifteen minutes outside of the city limits, Devon turns onto a side road just off the main highway. With the music down low, they can hear the gravel underneath the car heading to Devon's special place. The brownish green foliage has overtaken the side road. At the foot of the road, Devon parks the car at an angle close to the lake.

Looking out across the lake at the horizon, the sunset casts a heavenly glow. They can see the tiny ripples of water shimmering across the lake in the distance.

"Devon, this is beautiful," Tonya says.

He asks if he could interest her in taking a walk along side the lake. As they are walking, he can see that she is deep in thought. Devon asks her what has her so distracted.

She smiles and replies, "I am impressed. This is what I missed in my last relationship."

Devon sees a window of opportunity and is not going to let it close. The timing is perfect for him.

"I'm sorry to hear that. Did you have a bad experience in your last relationship?"

Tonya shrugs her shoulders. "It was all right, but we were too different. We knew it in the beginning, but for whatever reasons we decided to see if we could make it work. You know the saying 'opposites attract'? Well, that was not true for us. I saw us accomplishing goals and moving ahead, but he didn't see himself obtaining any of the goals I felt he could. I was there, giving him all the support he needed, but he couldn't see past next week."

Devon quickly interrupts. He wants to be the first one to put his feelings out in the open. "I know what you mean. I've been meeting all the wrong women for various reasons."

Tonya nods with understanding.

"Tonya, do you know of a place where a man can find a nice woman who is not about playing games and is ready to settle down? I put my heart and soul into my last relationship only to have her walk out of my life without any warning. But time has passed, and I have healed. I believe love is out there for me."

Devon turns to face Tonya and says, "I am looking to start a family, to leave work knowing there's someone at home who loves me as much as I love her and who can't wait to see me."

Devon grabs Tonya's hands, looks directly into her eyes, and says, "I want my next relationship to be one where when we look into each other's eyes, we hear those unspoken words because our souls are connected."

Tonya takes a minute to catch her breath. She is thinking, "Is this happening? Could it be true? A man who can communicate his thoughts and feelings about what he wants." Devon slowly releases Tonya's hands and takes a deep breath looking up, rubbing his hands down his face.

Devon takes another deep breath and says, "I'm sorry. What were we talking about before I went off into left field?"

Thinking with her heart, she takes hold of his hand, and with each word that spilled out of his mouth, she feels the pain he spoke about. "That's okay. It takes a real man to open up and tell someone how he feels."

"You caught me. I can be a little sensitive at times."

"Yeah, I see," she says with a smile on her face.

"Well, it's getting late, and we have one more workshop left this for weekend, thank God…Are you ready to go?"

"Yeah, you are right. Let's go."

On the way back to the hotel, grabbing his hand, Tonya intertwines their fingers and caresses his arm.

When they arrive back at the hotel, Devon looks to see if

Michelle is still at work as they walk through the foyer. She has already left for the evening.

Devon, being a gentleman, escorts Tonya to her room. After a friendly hug and a thank you for a wonderful evening, Devon wishes Tonya a good night.

While Devon is walking to his room, he reflects on how smooth he has been tonight and his brilliant last line to Tonya: "I want my next relationship to be one where when we look into each other's eyes, and we hear those unspoken words, because our souls are connected." Or something like that. *Damn, man, you are good! I've got to remember that one.* Devon feels he was a true gentleman tonight because he can picture Tonya in her room with her shoes kicked off, lying across the bed, hugging a pillow as if it was him. He knows that she is wondering if he could be "the one." After all, he gave her some of his best lines.

Once Devon makes it to his room, he cannot help

> "I WANT MY NEXT RELATIONSHIP TO BE ONE WHERE WHEN WE LOOK INTO EACH OTHER'S EYES, AND WE HEAR THOSE UNSPOKEN WORDS, BECAUSE OUR SOULS ARE CONNECTED."

thinking about Vanessa. He wants to know what she might be doing at this moment. In his room, walking over to the mini-bar, he thinks about the message that Michelle left for him earlier. After pouring himself a glass of coke, he takes out his phone, scrolling through his list of contacts, looking for Michelle's number. He ponders for a moment. "No, that's all right. She is really not my type," he says to himself. He places the phone on the night stand, reaches for the remote control, and lays down on the bed.

He takes a sip from the glass and places the glass on the nightstand. He channel-surfs for a sports channel, but when he does not find one, he gives up and decides to call it a night.

It is Sunday afternoon, and the conference is over. Devon stops in the middle of packing his bags when he decides to call Tonya to see if she needs help with her bags. Tonya's phone rings.

"Hello."

"Hey, you. I was calling to see if you would like for me to help you take your bags downstairs?"

"No, I have them, thanks. But you can meet me down-stairs in about fifteen minutes."

"Okay."

Devon continues packing his bags but also reflecting back over the weekend. *Well, another conference done came and gone again. I really didn't learn much at the meeting, but oh well. I have to say it was a good weekend. I met Tonya. She's a good girl. I didn't get laid I like I had plan, but I could have*

with Michelle...but na, she really isn't my type. But Vanessa on
the other hand...Boy. I would have...it's not over yet. There is
next week.

Devon zips the last bag he brought with him and heads
downstairs to the lobby. As he approaches the registration desk
to check out, he catches a glimpse of Vanessa outside getting
into a cab. Just then, Tonya walks up behind him and places her
hand on his back.

"Hey, Devon."

"Hey, you. I'm so glad to see you. Well, this is it."

"Yep."

"I'll give you a call when I get home and settles in. Now
come give me a hug, girl."

Later that night, he calls Tonya to keep her attention on
him. After an hour of small talk about the conference and the
weekend, Tonya, having an early day on Monday, tells Devon
she will talk with him the next day.

But there is still Vanessa.

Monday morning, Devon walks into his office. He sits
down at his desk and listens to the messages that were left over
from Friday. When he logs onto the computer, he notices an
email from Tonya thanking him for a wonderful weekend in
spite of the boring meetings they had to attend. Devon replies
back to Tonya's message hoping she will still be logged into an
instant messenger. He wants to keep Tonya's mind focused on

him. As he hoped, she is still logged in to an instant messenger service, and they are having a "live" conversation.

Ten minutes into their conversation, Devon's phone rings. He tells Tonya that he has to take a call but for her not to log out because he will be right back.

"Hello, Devon McNeil speaking."

"Hello, Mr. McNeil, my name is Susan. I am calling from Chambers Studios on behalf of Vanessa Lewis. She is requesting a meeting to discuss the transition of the accounting responsibility over to us. She has two openings—Tuesday at 11:00 a.m. or 3:00 p.m. Which one will work best with your schedule?"

"Please let Ms. Lewis know that 11:00 a.m. will be fine, and I look forward to meeting with her."

"Okay, Mr. McNeil. I will put it on her calendar."

Devon types in, "I'm Back," to let Tonya know he is ready to continue their conversation. Tonya asks Devon what his plans are for the evening and if he would like to meet her for dinner.

He replies, "That sounds great, but I am preparing for a very important meeting with a client. I will call you later tonight, okay?"

"…That's fine," she says.

Even though Devon finds Tonya very attractive, he is contemplating his strategy to win over Vanessa. He begins by stopping by the mall to pick up a few things.

It is about 9:00 p.m. when Devon makes it home from

shopping. He remembers that he has promised Tonya a call. He does not want to be on the phone for too long, so he dials the number with every intention of making it a five-minute conversation.

"Tonya, I'm sorry I didn't call you sooner, but I am still not finished with my reports. I wanted to at least give you a call before it got too late."

"That's all right," Tonya replies. "This must be one of your company's largest accounts."

"Yes, it is. We might be losing their business unless I can change their minds tomorrow."

"Devon, I know you will do fine."

"Thank you for the vote of confidence, Tonya. I really need to finish up and get ready for tomorrow."

"Okay, Devon. I will email you from work tomorrow."

Tuesday morning finally arrives. Devon decides to go straight to the meeting with Vanessa instead of going to his office first. As he sits in the lobby of Chambers Studios waiting for the receptionist to buzz Vanessa, he remembers that he has left something in the car. He runs out to get it before Vanessa comes down to meet him.

Rushing back into the building, Devon makes it just in time. Susan, Vanessa's secretary, has just come down to get him and bring him up to Vanessa's office. They get into the elevator, and Susan presses the button for the tenth floor. When Devon gets off the elevator, there stand two double doors at the end of the hallway. Walking towards the doors, he notices the elaborate artwork that drapes the walls.

Off to the side of the double doors is a sitting area and desk.

"Please have a seat, Mr. McNeil. Ms. Lewis will be out shortly," Susan says.

"Thanks."

Marveling at the thought of the size of her office, Devon takes a seat. The double doors open five minutes later, and Vanessa walks out. She's wearing a navy blue business suit.

"Hello again, Mr. McNeil."

"Please call me Devon," he offers with his out-stretched hand.

"Well, okay, Devon."

With a firm handshake, Vanessa invites Devon into her office to have a seat.

"As you are aware, the CFO has decided to bring the accounting in-house, which means we will no longer be using your services. Please understand this is not a reflection of your work. I have done my homework and found out that you have come highly recommended."

"Thank you, Vanessa. That being said, is there any way I can persuade your company to continue to work with us? Perhaps on a consulting basis."

Vanessa raises an eyebrow, but Devon is not deterred.

"Vanessa, the way I see it, we have been working with this company for over three years. We know the financial history in and out. Now, we are offering our consulting services so you won't have any down time as a result of the transition."

Vanessa leans back in her chair and ponders Devon's offer.

"Mr. McNeil, you make some very valid points. For the time being, I don't see why we cannot have you consult on some of the business actions. Please understand this is temporary and will end once we have our staff in place."

"I understand."

As the meeting ends, Devon notices that it is close to the lunch hour. *It's now or never*, he thinks to himself. So, he reaches into his bag, pulls out a small, white, furry stuffed Maltese dog and places it on Vanessa's desk next to her computer.

"I remember you telling me you missed Princess. I was in a little shop getting a gift for my mother's birthday this weekend when I saw this and thought about you. Until you are able to get back home to pick up Princess, you can just look to the left of your desk and know she is all right."

"Thank you. How thoughtful of you."

Devon can feel she is warming up to him. "Tell you what—it's about lunch time. Would you like to get something to eat?"

"I would love to, but I have lunch plans already. Thank you for the gift."

"Maybe next time."

"Listen, Devon. I appreciate the gift, and from what I have seen, I think you are an intelligent man and a nice person. I have to tell you up front that I am already involved with someone back home, and even though things aren't that great between us, I am still going to try and work things out."

"I fully understand. I hope things work out for you two. Please do not take my gesture the wrong way. I know that you are new in town, and I just wanted to get you something to welcome you to our lovely city."

"In that case, maybe we can do lunch sometime in the near future, as friends."

Devon drives to the office with a long face. He had hoped that things would have turned out differently after his meeting with Vanessa. By the time he finally gets back into the office, Tonya has sent him several messages already. As he sits down to check his email, he says to himself, *Oh, well! Let me go ahead and see what's up with Tonya for now, I know Vanessa will eventually come back around.*

Feeling a need for female companionship, Devon sends an email message to Tonya asking her out for dinner that night. Tonya accepts, and they agree to meet at a nearby Japanese restaurant at around 7:30 p.m.

Over dinner, Devon talks about his meeting and how it did not go as well as planned. He tells her that they will eventually lose the account, but right now he is just doing some consulting work until the transition is complete. Knowing that Tonya is a supportive and encouraging woman, and at that moment not caring about anybody except his own selfishness, he uses her vulnerability to his advantage.

"You know, Tonya, it's times like this when having a loving mate at home to listen to your problems, give you a back rub, and offer words of encouragement is what I need."

Before he can say another word, his cell phone rings. After looking at the caller ID, he asks Tonya to excuse him for a moment.

"Hello, Devon speaking."

On the other end of the phone, a sexy voice says, "Hi, Devon, this is Carol. Did I catch you at a bad time?"

"No, I am sitting here having dinner with Tonya. What's been up? I haven't talked to you in a while. If my memory serves me correctly, it's been about three months."

"You know why you haven't heard from me. I don't want to go into that right now. I just made it back from my trip, and I wanted to invite you over this evening."

"Okay!"

"I see you can't talk, so call me when you are on your way."

"I am having dinner right now with my lady friend, but you can tell me all about your trip later. Okay?"

Devon hangs up the phone and continues his conversation with Tonya. "Sorry about that, Tonya. That was my friend, Carol. I've known her for about seven, no eight, years now. She's been on vacation in St. Thomas and wants to tell me about her trip."

"No problem. I understand," Tonya says.

Little does Tonya know, Devon was actually arranging a

"booty call" for tonight. He made it seem as though it was a harmless conversation with an old friend. When he acknowledged that he is having dinner with a lady friend openly, it withdrew any red flags that Tonya might have had.

"That's what I like about you, you are so nurturing and understanding. It's hard to find a woman that doesn't sweat the small stuff. It's getting late, and I know you have to go to work in the morning. Thank you for making time for me. I really needed someone to talk to tonight."

"No problem. Anytime, Devon."

Devon motions the waiter to bring the check. After paying for dinner, Devon walks Tonya to her car. He kisses her on her forehead and tells her to drive safely. He asks her to call him after she makes it home.

Before Devon can get the key in the ignition, he shouts the name Carol. The voice controlled navigation system dials Carol's home number. Her phone rings.

"Hello."

"Hey, girl, this is Devon, your lover man. I will be there in about twenty minutes."

He ends the call with Carol and immediately dials Tonya's number. Devon knows that Tonya wants to have one last conversation with him tonight. By the time Tonya would call Devon, he would already be at Carol's house and unable to talk to Tonya in-depth. So he initiates the final call for tonight.

Tonya answers her phone.

"Hello."

"Hey, you, it's Devon. I know I told you to call me when you made it home, but I couldn't wait any longer, so I decided to call you first."

"Devon, are you at home already?"

"No, but I am not far."

"Okay, well, I have just turned into my driveway. I'm safe and sound."

"Okay, I know you have an early day tomorrow, so do me a favor?"

"What's that, Devon?"

"I just want you to think about me tonight," he requests with laughter in his voice. "Sweet dreams!"

…It's playtime…

When Devon arrives at Carol's, he strolls in as if he owns the place. Carol is in the living room watching T.V.

"I see you left the door unlocked for me. What do you have to drink?"

Devon gets a beer out of the refrigerator, opens it, and then sits down next to Carol on the couch.

"Who is Tonya? Your new girlfriend?" Carol says.

"No! I just met her last weekend."

"You haven't changed, I see. When are you going to settle down and stop being a player?"

"When the time is right. You want a man to be for real when he settles down, right? Once I get all my playing out, then I'll settle down. But until then, come and give Big Daddy a kiss."

Devon and Carol have been in this love triangle for eight

years. Carol calls Devon periodically to check up on him to see how he's doing. Carol started out in the same place as Tonya, but Carol decided one day that enough was enough. She was tired of playing the waiting game, trying to stick it out with Devon hoping he would change. So now, whenever she's not in a relationship and feels like being with a man, she calls Devon.

Carol gets up and straddles Devon, runs her hands down his chest, and gives him a very sexual, open-mouthed kiss. Devon wraps his strong arms around Carol's body, pressing his muscular chest next to hers as he stands up. Carol drapes her arms and legs around Devon as he walks into the master bedroom.

The next morning at work, Devon sits at his desk wondering what Vanessa might be doing. He wants to call but knows that that would not be a good move on his part. His thoughts shift to Tonya. *It is time to speed things up a little. How can I get Tonya to my house tonight? Oh! I know.* He logs on to the instant messenger to see if she is there.

"Hey, you," he writes. "Are you there? I was just touching base to say hello. I have a real busy day today and I am also leaving early, so give me a call tonight."

Tonya replies within seconds, "Okay, I will give you a call later this evening. Have a nice day."

On the way home, Devon stops by the grocery store to pick up a few things. Seven o'clock rolls around, and his plan is in full motion. As he arrives at home, his phone is ringing. He looks at the caller ID and answers, "Hello, Tonya."

"How did you know it was me? You must have been looking at your Caller ID. How are you doing?"

"I am all right; just winding down from the day."

"What are you doing? I hear a lot of noise in the background."

"I decided to cook a little something—nothing special, though."

"Oh, really. What are you cooking?"

"Some lemon-peppered chicken breasts, pasta, and garlic bread."

"Sounds good," Tonya says.

"Well, I planned on taking my lunch tomorrow, so I made more than enough for me. You are more than welcome to stop by and try some, if you would like."

"I guess I can run through for a minute. Where do you live?"

"Are you familiar with Autum Brook Mall?"

"Yes."

"Well, call me once you make it to the mall, and I will give you directions from there."

Devon picks up the ready-made, lemon-peppered chicken dinner he purchased earlier. All he has to do now is pop it in the oven and warm it up. He deliberately messes up a few pots and chops some onions and green peppers. He also takes some seasoning out of the cabinets to make it seem as if he has been cooking for a while. The phone rings. It is Tonya calling to get directions. He tells her his address and explains how to get there. About five minutes later, the doorbell rings. Devon opens the door and welcomes Tonya to his home.

"You look good, girl."

"Thank you," she replies. "The food smells good."

"Dinner will be ready in about five minutes. Have a seat, relax, and make yourself at home."

Devon brings Tonya a glass of wine. He walks into the dining room and lights candles on the dining room table. He calls out for Tonya to join him. "Dinner is ready. Come and have a seat in the dining room. Do you need to wash your hands?"

"Yes."

"The bathroom is the first door down the main hallway on the right-hand side."

Back in the dining room, Devon is lighting the last candle, thinking to himself, *I know Tonya likes the way I decorated my bathroom, and that peach fragrance smells good.*

When Tonya walks back into the living, the first thing she says is, "Devon, I am impressed. You keep a very clean bathroom for a man."

I know. That gets them every time. Hmph, he thinks.

"Devon, the food looks good."

"I hope it tastes as good as it looks," Devon says.

"Wow, you didn't tell me you could cook."

"I can do a little something in the kitchen."

"You are funny! Devon, I can cook a little, but nothing like this. My style of cooking goes as far as Hamburger

Helper."

"Hey, there is nothing wrong with that. I eat it sometimes myself."

After dinner, Devon suggests that they go into the den to finish their wine and listen to some music. Tonya makes herself comfortable on the floor with her back against the love seat. Devon decides to sit on the love seat behind her. He enters "56" on the stereo's remote control. He wants to hear one of his favorite slow jam CDs.

Tonya is in the middle of a sentence when Devon suddenly places his hands on her shoulders and begins to rub her back.

"That feels good! I could use a back rub."

Even though Tonya seems to be a good woman and could possibly make a good wife, for right now, Devon's main interest is to add Tonya to his list of casual sex partners without commitment.

Caught up in the feeling of Devon's strong but soft hands relaxing her tense muscles, her guard is down, and Devon figures it is the perfect time to test the waters. He leans over and kisses her on her neck. He quickly apologizes for his behavior and tells Tonya he could not resist. He hopes that she will say it is okay. After a moment of silence, Tonya turns around, captures his lips, and explores his mouth in an arousing, purely lustful kiss. Before long, there is a trail of clothes leading to the master bedroom.

The next morning, Tonya has a hard time concentrating on work-related activities. She keeps slipping into thoughts of the night before. It had been a fervent and erotic night of passion. She sends an email message to Devon and tells him how she feels. Devon replies, "…It was great for me, too."

Over the next several weeks, they see each other regularly.

One Saturday afternoon, while riding in the car with Devon, Tonya asks in what direction their relationship is headed. Devon hesitates. He knows he needs to say something quickly to get her off the subject.

"What? You don't want to be with me anymore? Oh, I know. You're mad at me because I didn't call you back last night. I'm sorry. I fell asleep, okay?"

"No, Devon, I just want to make sure we are both looking for the same thing."

"Tonya, let me ask you this. Do you like spending time with me?"

"Yes."

"I enjoy spending time with you as well. I feel we get along great with each other. We have a lot in common. Why should we worry about all that? We should just continue to do what we have been doing these last several weeks and let the rest fall into place. Now lean over here and give me a kiss."

Devon thinks that even though he has made it through this interrogation without being burned, he needs to do something that will prevent this line of questioning for a while. Knowing that Tonya will bring it up again, Devon does the only thing he can think of to make Tonya believe that he is being truthful. Fifteen minutes later, they pull into a driveway.

"Whose house is this?" Tonya asks.

He replies, "You'll see."

A little uneasy with where they are, she walks behind Devon. When they get to the door, Devon takes out a key and opens it. "Mom! Mom! Come here! I want you to meet someone."

"Mom!" Tonya's eyes widen as all kinds of mixed feelings and thoughts run through her head.

"Boy! Here I come," Devon's mother says.

"Mom, I want you to meet Tonya Williams."

"Hello, baby, how are you doing?" his mom asks. "She is pretty, Devon. Where did you meet her?"

"At a business function."

"Devon, you know your brother Tim is coming home within the next couple of weeks."

"Yes, I know, Mom."

"Well, have you two eaten?"

"No," Devon answers.

"Good, because I just finished cooking. Devon, show Tonya where she can wash up and then you can come help me for a second."

Devon leads Tonya down the hallway and into the bathroom. He turns on the light and asks if she is okay. Tonya assures him that she is fine, and he leans down and gives her kiss.

Devon closes the door and walks back into the kitchen where his mother is taking cornbread out of the oven.

"Boy, when are you going to settle down? This is the fourth girl you have brought over here this year, and it is not even May."

"Mom, you know how it is. I can't settle down just yet. I am enjoying the single life too much."

"No, baby, I don't! I did not raise you that way. I raised you to respect women and treat them how you would treat me. I was afraid this would happen."

"What would happen?"

"That you would grow up to be like that no good…I mean, like your daddy." Devon laughs, because he knows his father very well.

"Mom! When I am ready, I am going to settle down."

The bathroom door squeaks as it opens, and Devon tells his mom, "Shh…keep it down. Tonya is coming." Tonya walks into the kitchen.

"Mrs. McNeil, something smells really good."

"Thank you," Mrs. McNeil says, "Now come sit down, and I'll fix a plate for you. I assume you like seasoned pork chops, mashed potatoes and gravy with hot cornbread, and cinnamon apples."

"Yes, Mrs. McNeil, thank you. I see where Devon gets his cooking skills."

Mrs. McNeil smiles as she glances over at her son. Devon has a look on his face like, "Mom, you better not say anything." He recalls a previous time when he brought another one of his lady friends over. She asked his mom did she teach Devon how to cook and his mom said, "I know Devon didn't give you one of those pre-cooked meals and told you he fixed it. Did he? Lord have mercy."

Devon wants to hurry up and get off this subject, so he asks Tonya to pass the cornbread.

After they finish eating, Devon tells his mother that he needs to get going because he has to buy some new basketball shoes for his game tomorrow.

"It was nice meeting you, Tonya. Hope to see you again."

"Likewise, Mrs. McNeil. Thank you so much for the meal."

While they are riding, Tonya expresses how surprised she had been when she realized that he had taken her to meet his mom and how she wished she had known so she could have fixed herself up a little more. Devon reassures Tonya that his mother likes her and feels she is a very nice person.

Curious about his intentions, Tonya asks Devon why he didn't tell her they were stopping by his mom's house.

Devon looks at her with a half smile and simply says, "I wanted you to meet her, that's all."

Tonya is speechless. She really does not know what to think or how to react. Most guys will take only a girl they really care for to meet their mothers. Tonya is feeling secure in her relationship with Devon and kisses him on the cheek. She settles back into the seat and enjoys the ride with whom she considers her soon-to-be man.

"Hey, baby, I need to stop by the mall if you don't mind."

"That's cool, Devon! I want to look at some pants anyway."

At the mall, Devon stops by two stores that sell basketball shoes before deciding on a pair. Meanwhile, Tonya walks around looking at the new fall apparel. They meet at the food court where they stop for ice cream and then prepare to leave the mall. Devon takes Tonya's hand as they walk through the mall and eat their ice cream. Devon notices a ring in a jewelry store window. He tugs Tonya's hand to get her attention.

"Baby, do you like that ring?"

Not thinking anything of it, Tonya looks at the ring and replies nonchalantly, "It's nice."

"Let's go in and look around for a minute," Devon says.

Once in the store, Tonya lets go of Devon's hand and walks over to the tennis bracelets. Looking at a sparkling, diamond-lined bracelet, Tonya asks the salesperson if she can try it on.

"Devon, what do you think? You like it?"

"Yeah, it's nice, but come here for a minute. I want to show you something. What do you think of it?"

Devon stands holding a 2-carat diamond ring between his thumb and index finger.

"Try it on and see if it fits. Do you like it, Tonya?"

"YES!"

"What are your finance options?" Devon asks the salesperson.

He informs Devon that he can apply for a store credit card

and remarks that they make a perfect couple. At that moment, Tonya looks at Devon.

He turns to the salesperson and says, "This is the first store we've been to. We are going to look at some other stores before making a decision."

As they leave the jewelry store, Devon places his hand around Tonya's waist and kisses her on her forehead. Once back in the car, Devon thinks to himself, *Man, that was a close one. But that should buy me at least three to four months before this conversation will come up again. By then, I should know what I want to do about Tonya.*

…STILL Vanessa…

Monday morning Devon is sitting at his desk chatting with Tonya on the instant messenger when his phone rings. He messages Tonya that he has a call and will be back in a minute and not to log off.

"Hello, Devon McNeil speaking."

"Mr. McNeil, this is Vanessa Lewis with Chambers Studios."

"Please! Call me Devon."

"Okay, Devon, I have a 2:00 p.m. meeting over in your area and thought I might give you a call to see if you wanted to meet for lunch to go over the progress of the transition. I know it's been close to two months since we last spoke."

"Sure! I know a great Mediterranean restaurant not far from here. Since you are still new to the area, I will email you directions on how to get there."

"Okay. I'll meet you, let's say, around noon."

"Sounds good. I'll see you then."

Devon hangs up the phone and in a whispered tone says, "Thank you."

He leans back in his chair and thinks about what he is going to do or say to get Vanessa to realize that, even though she has a man, she might be missing out on a good thing with him.

Okay, Devon, man, you have just been handed another chance. Let's see what you are going to do with it. Come on, playa, let those creative juices flow, he thinks to himself.

"Damn! I forgot about Tonya." He logs back into the instant messenger. "Hey, you, I'm back. Did you miss me? Sorry it took so long. Guess who was on the phone?"

"Yes, Devon, of course, I missed you. It's okay. I had some reports I had to print. So who was on the phone?"

"Ed McMahon, and I won the sweepstakes," he laughs. "No, girl, it was Chambers Studios. They want to meet today for lunch. I know we had plans, but I promise to make it up to you."

"Don't worry about that. This is a good sign. Just continue to pray about it and have faith. Everything will work out just like you want."

"Well, baby, it's about 11:30. I need to get going so I won't be late. Call you tonight. Have a good day."

"Good luck. I will talk to you later."

Devon arrives at the restaurant a few minutes early, hoping to get a seat next to the waterfall. "Hello, sir! Would you like a table or would you prefer to sit at the bar?"

"No, a table for two will be fine. Do you have a table near the waterfall?"

"Yes, would you like to be seated?"

"You can go ahead and seat me, but a client will be joining me for lunch. Oh! By the way, my name is Mr. McNeil, and she may ask for me by name, but I will keep an eye out for her."

Devon makes sure he sits in the chair facing the door so he will not miss Vanessa. He notices her when she walks through the door. She is standing there talking to the hostess.

Devon watches as Vanessa is escorted to the table. He stands, walks around to the empty chair, and pulls it out for her.

"Hello, Vanessa. I hope you found the place okay."

"Yes, thank you. The directions were great."

"I would have taken the liberty of ordering wine, but I wasn't sure that you would like wine with lunch."

"That would have been fine. I need one after the day I've been having so far."

"What's going on, if you don't mind my asking?"

"Well, we are being audited. This is no reflection on the work your company has done. In fact, the records that your company has kept may help us out. You see, Jim, the CFO, is under investigation. I am meeting with him and some investors this afternoon, and he doesn't know about it yet."

"I know everything will work out for you. If there is anything I can do to help out, please let me know."

"I'm sure I will be calling on you, but right now I would just like to enjoy a glass of wine, some good food, and good company."

"No problem. Have you been home to pick Princess up yet?"

"Yes, I went home last weekend for the first time."

"Well, that was good timing. I heard they had a big jazz festival this past weekend."

"Yeah! But I didn't go this year."

"You mean your man didn't take you to the concerts?"

Devon wants to know how Vanessa's relationship is going before he plays his cards.

"Oh, no! We are not seeing each other anymore. I have to concentrate on my career. My life and career are here now, and his life is in Atlanta. One of us would have to make a change. I really like what I do, so my moving back to Atlanta is definitely out of the question."

"I'm sorry to hear that. Well, Vanessa, some men can't handle women who are more successful than they are. It interferes with their male egos. The man is the breadwinner. Many men will feel insecure and threatened by a woman in your position. That type of man thinks that since a woman is able to support herself, she will not need him anymore."

"Well, you are probably right. But if you ask me, I think that's silly. A man should want a woman to be his equal, especially with the economy like it is."

Vanessa is providing Devon with even more ammunition

to help bring her down. He now knows a couple of more things that he could do to further distinguish himself from the last guy Vanessa was with.

The waiter stops and asks them if they are ready to order. Vanessa orders Mediterranean Shrimp Pasta, and Devon orders Marinated Loin of Lamb. Shortly, the food is delivered to their table.

While eating, Devon asks, "Have you been to the Arts District downtown?"

"No. Why?"

"A friend of mine owns a place near downtown, and there is an open mic event tonight. Sometimes you can even catch our homegrown artists performing. Would you like to go?"

"What time does it start?" she asks, seeming interested.

"The open mic starts about 8:00 p.m."

"That sounds like fun."

"Since you are not too familiar with the area, I can meet you somewhere and you can follow me there if you would like."

"You can just pick me up about 7:30 p.m. at my place."

"Okay."

Vanessa is enjoying Devon's company. He can tell from her body language. She is sitting in her chair with an inviting posture, and she isn't holding back the laughs anymore.

In the midst of their conversation, the waiter comes by their table with the dessert tray. The dessert prompts Vanessa to inquire about the time. Looking down at her watch, she checks to see what time it is.

"Oh, I have to run. I am going to be late, but here is my address, and if you get lost, call me at home." She writes down her home number for him.

After seeing Vanessa off, Devon gets back into his car and thinks about the conversation they had while driving back to work. *Man, that guy Vanessa was with sounds weak. I would love to have a strong woman who can stand on her own...That just means I don't have to carry the full load all the time. It would be nice to have someone spend some of their money on me for a change.*

Devon heads back to the office. He finishes work early so he can leave and get ready for his outing with Vanessa.

He sends an email message to Tonya to let her know the details about his meeting at lunch. He tells her that he will be working late pulling files and preparing information to give to the client.

On his way home, he stops at a grocery store to pick up some shaving cream. While walking the aisles, he runs into Samantha, one of his ex-opponents from earlier in the year. Samantha had decided it was in her best interests to end their so-called relationship. She rightly felt there was no chance that Devon would change his ways and commit to a relationship with her. Seeing him again brings back a lot of old feelings and desires, though.

"Hello, Devon. How are you doing these days?"

"I'm fine. I haven't heard from you in a while."

"No, you haven't, but we both know why."

"I see you are still looking good!"

"Thanks. You, too. Devon, this is my girlfriend, Kathy."

"Hello, Kathy. It's nice to meet you."

"Likewise."

"Devon, do you still have the same number? I may give you a call sometime."

"Don't keep me waiting by the phone for your call."

"I'm sure you won't be waiting by the phone with all those ladies chasing you."

"Hey! That's not true. You know there will always be a place in my heart for you."

"I see you haven't changed. Bye, Devon."

As she turns and walks away, Devon takes a long look at her body and reminisces about those long nights of passion. After a thirty-second pause, he remembers why he came to the store. "I need to pick up some shaving cream." But as he's about to turn and walk away, he sees the women slap high-five and laugh. His suspicions get the best of him. He wants to know what they are talking about, so he waits on the other side of the aisle to catch a piece of their conversation.

"Samantha, Devon is fine."

"He is fine. Fine as they come."

"So what happened, girl?"

"Devon isn't any different than every other man out there. He's a dog."

"Tell me about it, but I don't remember you telling me

about him."

"Girl, it wasn't anything."

"So what happened?"

"First of all I met Devon a couple of months ago at Platinum when you were out of town visiting your mother. I made the mistake of going home with him that night, but it was good at first."

"Okay, keep going," Kathy says, stopping in the middle of the aisle so Samantha can tell her the full story.

"He knows how to treat a woman. He made me feel special, like the world revolved around me. Showing me with attention and telling me stories of how he was ready for a serious relationship."

"Go on."

"What else is there to say accept when I saw past his little tricks, I let him go."

"But was the sex good?"

"That's the one thing I miss about that man," Samantha says shaking her head.

Devon has heard all he needs to hear. He walks away looking for the shaving cream. Devon finds the shaving cream he is looking for, and as he makes his way toward the check-out lines, he remembers a move that might position him closer to capturing Vanessa's heart. He changes his route and locates the greeting cards aisle. He chooses a card that is blank inside. He thinks a card would be perfect for that night. He goes back to the check-out and pays for the items.

He arrives home and immediately showers, shaves, and dresses. Then, he opens the blank card and writes a few thoughts to Vanessa.

He makes it to Vanessa's house and rings the doorbell.

"Hi, Devon," she says, as she opens the door.

"Hello, Vanessa! You look lovely tonight."

"Thank you."

"You ready?" he asks.

"Sure, let me get my purse."

In the car, he turns down the music so they can talk. "I hope you don't mind the surroundings. The place we are going is very down-to-earth. It has a peaceful feel to it. I forgot to mention there are no chairs. We will sit on pillows. There are all kinds of artwork on the walls. I like to go there when I want to get away and be around positive individuals."

They arrive at LYRICAL CAFÉ. As they walk in, Vanessa looks around. She wants to get a feel for the people. While they stand waiting, a woman approaches them and welcomes them to Poetry Night. She embraces Vanessa with a huge hug and leads them to an open space on the café floor. She explains that the poetry reading will begin in about ten minutes.

Vanessa turns to Devon and says, "You were right. This place does make you feel at peace. I feel very comfortable. I'm glad we came."

"I'm glad you like it."

Devon thinks the ambiance and the seating arrangement will allow him to get a little closer to Vanessa. Devon excuses himself and goes to the men's room before the first set. While in the men's room, he takes out his phone and calls Tonya.

"Hey, you! Are you in bed yet?"

"Not yet."

"I just wanted to talk to you for a minute before you fall asleep. I just finished the reports that Chambers needs. I am excited because they might decide to keep my company on board if this information saves them. I will let you rest now… I will email you in the morning."

Devon returns to find Vanessa consumed with the passionate words that pour from the lips of a fervent poet telling his tale of unrequited love.

"I'm back! Do you want something to drink?"

"No, I'm okay. Thanks." Vanessa repositions the pillows to support Devon's back and unexpectedly snuggles underneath his arm. "Hmm," he says, looking down at Vanessa with a smile on his face. About an hour later, the last poet finishes his lyrical rhythm, and they leave.

"Did you enjoy yourself?" Devon asks.

"Surprisingly, yeah, I did. Thanks for inviting me," Vanessa smiles, delighted.

Before she slides into the car, she stops and gives him a kiss on the cheek.

They return to Vanessa's house. He gets out of the car but first reaches inside the door panel and retrieves the card he picked up earlier. He opens the passenger door, helps Vanessa out of the car, and escorts her to the front door. He gives her a hug and kisses her on her cheek before wishing her a good night. He slides the card in her coat pocket while they are hugging. He makes sure the card is not too far in and that it is in a place where it will fall out easily. He walks back to his car and heads home.

Vanessa closes the door, kicks off her shoes, places her purse on the counter top, and lays her coat across the barstool. She thinks about how much she has enjoyed the evening out with Devon and reaches for the phone to check her messages. She notices an envelope on the floor underneath her coat. While she checks messages, she picks up the envelope, which is addressed to her. She opens the envelope, curious to know when and from where it came. The outside reads, "Just Because." There is a background picture of a moonlit sky shadowing a city skyline. She opens the envelope and the enclosed card and finds a handwritten message. *Hello! Vanessa, I hope you enjoyed this evening as much as I did. I felt from the conversations we had earlier today that tonight would be special. I just want to thank you for a wonderful evening, and I hope to see you again on a personal level. Sweet dreams! Devon McNeil.*

Not sure what to say, she picks up the phone and calls him. "Hi, Devon. This is Vanessa."

"Hi, Vanessa. Is everything okay?"

"Yes, of course! I just found the card. How sweet! I enjoyed myself tonight as well, and, yes, we can see each other again outside of work."

"I'm glad you liked it. Well, good night and sweet dreams."

The following morning at work, Tonya's phone rings. It is Devon on the other end.

"This is Tonya."

"Hey, you, good morning. How are you doing?"

"Fine, now that I am speaking to you. Did you get everything finished last night?"

"Yeah, I was up pretty late trying to complete these files, but I think I may have gathered enough information for them to use."

"Devon, come by tonight, and I promise to take your mind off Chambers Studios."

"Um, yeah, I can do that. Well, I have some calls to make. I will hit you later on the instant messenger."

As the day progresses, Devon cannot stop thinking about his date last night. He feels Vanessa had a good time listening to the poetry because of the way she snuggled up against him, and the card was pure brilliance. He has to give himself a pat on the back for being so smooth.

Time seems to pass slowly. The moment the clock strikes five, Devon heads home to freshen up before going to Tonya's house. On his way home, his cell phone rings.

"Hello, this is Devon."

"Hi, Devon. This is Vanessa. How are you doing today?"

"Hey, Vanessa. I'm fine. What's going on?"

"Well, if you weren't busy, I wanted to invite you to happy

hour at Sherrods."

"Sure! I would love to. I will meet you there in about twenty minutes."

Devon hangs up the phone. He is thinking to himself, *Man, it doesn't get much better than this.* He already has one woman right where he wants her and is about to add Vanessa to that list of casual sex partners. Devon looks at his watch and figures he has about a three-hour window to make it over to Tonya's house before she will start calling his cell phone.

When he arrives at Sherrod's, he strides confidently to the bar to see if Vanessa has arrived. Finally, he gazes down the long bar and sees her sitting alone, looking appealing as usual. He walks over to her, rubbing his hands together and smiles. "I am about to get this one, too," he says to himself. He switches his phone to vibrate so the ringer will not interrupt his time with Vanessa.

They are having a few drinks and some laughs when Devon looks at his watch and realizes that two-and-a-half hours have passed. He apologizes to Vanessa for having to leave, and explains that it has been a long day for him and the next day will be even longer. Of course, he does not mention that in about ten minutes Tonya will probably be calling him.

As he walks Vanessa to her car, his cell phone begins to vibrate. He knows it is Tonya. He needs to get away quickly, so he opens Vanessa's car door and gives her a hug.

"Vanessa, give me a call when you get home," Devon says before he closes her door. She smiles and nods.

After he waves good-bye to Vanessa, he pulls out his cell phone and calls Tonya back.

"Hello."

"Hey, you."

"Devon! I thought you were coming over tonight."

"I am. I just had to stop by Sherrod's for happy hour with some business partners to have a drink, but I am on my way over right now."

"Okay. I'll see you when you get here."

Devon hangs up with Tonya and dials Vanessa's cell phone.

"Hello, Vanessa. I know I told you to call me when you make it home, but I wanted to hear your voice one last time. I am about ten minutes from the house, and I know the minute I walk through the door I am going straight to bed."

"I understand, Devon. I am tired myself. I am only two blocks away anyway. Be careful getting home."

"I will call you tomorrow after my morning meeting, and maybe we can get together this weekend."

At Tonya's house, she has prepared for a nice, romantic evening with Devon. She has even purchased a silky thin, spaghetti-strapped teddy from Victoria Secret. She places two champagne glasses in front of the fireplace and sets candles in strategic places around the room. Soft music fills the room. Just as she sprays sweet-scented Mari all over her body, the doorbell rings.

When Tonya opens the door wearing her new teddy,

Devon pauses for minute, not sure what to say or do. But he knows one thing for sure—tonight is going to be something out of the ordinary. In the house, barely standing in the living room, he turns to Tonya and says, "I wasn't expecting all of this."

"I know. I just wanted to help you relax a little. That's all."

He sits down on one of the pillows that Tonya has arranged on the floor in front of the fireplace as she fills the empty glasses with champagne. He sips his drink while Tonya slowly runs her fingers down his back. She suggests that he take off his shirt so she can give him a back rub. He unbuttons his shirt and lays down across the floor. Tonya pours massage oil in her palms and rubs his back and shoulders. After she is sure that Devon is relaxed, she lowers her mouth to his back and runs her warm tongue down the length of it. With that, the evening quickly progresses.

Devon awakens the next morning and looks over to see Tonya still sleeping. He kisses her on her forehead and rolls out of bed. He gathers his clothes and dresses, then lets himself out

SHE WAS HOLDING BACK ON ME, HE THINKS, RUBBING HIS HEAD, FEELING OVERWHELMED. HE DID NOT KNOW SHE COULD WORK IT LIKE THAT. *YOU NEVER KNOW! LOOKS CAN BE DECEIVING.*

159

the front door. On his way home, Devon is overcome with mixed emotions. He reevaluates his outlook on relationships. He mentally analyzes what happened last night and slowly becomes aware of the fact that the last night was one of the best he has had in a while, both mentally and especially physically. *She was holding back on me*, he thinks, rubbing his head, feeling overwhelmed. He did not know she could work it like that. *You never know! Looks can be deceiving.* His mind churns.

Later that day at work, he calls Tonya. "Hey, you, I was just sitting here thinking about you and wondering if you had any plans this weekend. I was thinking we could get away to a secluded place in the mountains, away from the hustle and bustle of city life. What do you say?" Tonya has done what no other woman has been able to do up until this point—"rock Devon's world." The brick wall that has shielded his heart finally has a crack in it, and Tonya is on the verge of tearing it down.

"That sounds good! When do you want to leave?"

"How long will it take you to get packed and ready? I'm thinking I will be there to pick you up around 7:30 p.m."

"Okay. I'll see you then."

After he hangs up with Tonya, his cell phone rings.

"Talk to me!" he says.

"Hello, Devon."

"Yeah! Who is this?"

"This is Samantha. After seeing you the other day, I wanted to see if you were available tonight."

"I'm sorry. I already have plans for tonight. Maybe some other time."

Samantha doesn't take the rejection very well.

"You must be going over to one of your other friend's houses tonight."

"No, and for your information, I am going away to the mountains this weekend with a very special lady in my life. So if that's all you want, I will talk to you another time."

Samantha hangs up the phone in disgust.

Devon arrives at Tonya's right at 7:30 p.m. She opens the door to let him in.

"Devon, have a seat. I will be ready in ten minutes."

As Devon walks away, Tonya notices something.

"Hey! What's that behind your back?"

"There's nothing behind my back. What are you talking about?"

"You know what I am talking about. What is that sticking out of your pants in the back?"

He reaches behind his back and pulls out a long-stemmed, red rose.

"You mean this? It's a single, long-stemmed red rose that is symbolic of my love for you. And as long as my heart beats and warm blood flows through my veins, there will always be a rose here to remind you of my commitment to you."

"Oh! How sweet."

"Now find a vase to put your rose in and a place where you can see it every time you come home."

Devon and Tonya load up the car and head to Devon's cabin in the mountains. Once they arrive, Devon unpacks the car while Tonya looks around. She wants to see the view of the valley down below. Inside the cabin, Devon lights the fireplace to give the cabin a warm and cozy feeling.

Devon grabs his cell phone and turns it off. Then he reaches for Tonya's cell phone. She eyes him suspiciously as if to say, "Give me back my phone."

"Tonya, I would like to spend this weekend alone with you—no people, no phones, no interruptions at all."

He turns, grabs her, and kisses her slowly and passionately. He tells her he wants to relive the night before.

It's about 5:00 p.m. Sunday evening, and Devon hates to leave, having been consumed with Tonya's love for the past two days. But Monday morning is rolling around and they must leave in order to make it back in time for work. During the drive back, Devon asks her if she would prefer a fall or a spring wedding. She is shocked by the question, but remains calm and says, "When that time comes, I would prefer a spring wedding."

"Good. I do, too," he says.

On Monday morning, Devon walks into his office, sits down, and reads the sticky note that is on his desk. He remembers he has forgotten to turn back on his cell phone when he made it back last night. When he turns it on, right away he hears three beeps, which are an indication that there are messages.

The first message was at 9:45 p.m. Friday night from

Samantha: "Hi, Devon, I'm sorry if I got upset, but I do want to see you this weekend if you're not too busy. Give me a call on my cell. Talk to you later." The second message was at 12:45 p.m. on Saturday. "Hi, Devon! This is Vanessa. I tried to reach you at home. I was calling to see if we are still on for tonight. Give me a call back when you get this message." Third message at 3:45 p.m. Saturday from Tim. "What's up, boy, this is your brother. I am at Mom's house. I will be here for two weeks. Hit me up when you get this message. But if I know my younger brother, you are probably laying up somewhere with some woman. But call me ASAP! Holla."

Devon hangs up the phone and calls his brother at home. Tim answers.

"What's up, Tim?"

"What's up, Devon?"

"Nothing much, just sitting here at the office. I am sorry I didn't call you over the weekend, but I spent the weekend with my lady friend."

"Well, that doesn't surprise me. I know how you do it."

"Tim, I think things are changing for me. I think I am ready to settle down now and be more like you."

"Not you! The one who said the only thing worse than getting married is laying in bed with a girl and you can't get a hard-on. Not my lil' brother."

"I am serious. I am for real this time. I tell you what. I am going to stop by this evening and bring her with me. Bet! Tell Momma I am coming by this evening and tell her I have a taste for some of her good cooking."

After hanging up the phone, he then emails Tonya. He tells her that his brother is in town and invites her to go with him to his mom's house after work. Tonya emails back and explains that she would love to meet his brother. They agree to meet at his place around 6:00 p.m. While he is watching the clock, wishing it were 5:00 p.m., Devon's desk phone rings.

"Devon McNeil speaking."

"Hi, Devon. This is Vanessa!"

"Hey there, pretty lady. I got your message over the weekend. I'm sorry for not returning your call, but my brother is in town, so I was entertaining this past weekend."

"That's okay, Devon, but you could have called and told me that."

"You know, you are right. I should have called you, but Vanessa, sometimes you can't see the forest for the trees."

"What are you talking about?"

"I mean you spend all your time looking for that special person, but all along they are right there next to you. I guess what I am trying

"I ENJOYED THE TIME YOU AND I SPENT TOGETHER, BUT I HATE TO SAY THIS...I WOULD PREFER IF WE ONLY SEE EACH OTHER ON A PROFESSIONAL LEVEL."

164

to say is that I realized a special someone has been right here all along. I enjoyed the time you and I spent together, but I hate to say this…I would prefer if we only see each other on a professional level."

"What? I hate the decision you made, but I can respect it. I wish you two the best."

"Thank you, Vanessa. I wish you the best as well."

Later at Devon's mother's house, his brother is standing in the driveway when Devon drives up with Tonya in the car.

He jumps out to give his brother a hug. "Tim, what's up, man?"

"Good to see you."

"Hey, Tim, this is Tonya, the one I was telling you about."

"Hey, Tonya! Nice to meet you."

"Nice to meet you, too, Tim."

"Mom, Devon and Tonya are here."

"Come in here and give your momma a hug."

"Momma, you remember Tonya, right?"

"Sure I do! Hello, Tonya."

"Hello, Mrs. McNeil. Nice to see you again."

"Well, come on in. I cooked Tim's favorite. Smothered pork chops with mashed potatoes, green beans and cheesecake."

"That sounds good, Mrs. McNeil."

"Child, call me Mom. Remember, Mom. Okay? Go and wash your hands so we can eat."

At the dinner table, Mom asks Devon to bless the food.

Caressing Tonya's hand, Devon starts to pray.

"Dear heavenly Father, thank You for this food we are about to receive. I pray that it will nourish our bodies. And dear heavenly Father, I thank You for allowing Tim to make it here safely and thank You for Mom, for enabling her to fix this wonderful meal for the nourishment of our bodies. I also would like to thank You for allowing me to realize the blessing You have given me. In Jesus name I pray, Amen.

...Yeah, right... Reality Check...

If we lived in a world where fairytales come true, then this would have been the perfect ending, but since most of us don't live in a world like that, here's what really happens.

Back to the morning after Tonya greets Devon at the door with nothing on but a teddy. Devon wakes up the next morning in Tonya's bed. He looks over to see her still sleeping. He kisses her on her forehead and rolls out of the bed. Not wanting to wake her, he gathers his clothes and dresses. He looks at Tonya once more before leaving.

While he is driving home, he analyzes what happened the night before, thinking that it had been one of the best nights he has had in a while. He knew all along that she had some freak in her. He was just waiting for it to come out.

Later that morning, Devon walks into his office, returns a couple of business calls, and then sits back in his chair planning the weekend. He thinks about the night with Tonya and decides to log in to the instant messenger to see if she left him any message this morning. Sure enough, there is one waiting for him. "Hey, you, I was hoping to see this morning before you left. I was just sitting here thinking about last night and wanting to thank you for a wonderful evening. I really needed for us to bond..."

He mentions to her that his brother will be coming into town this weekend, but also explains that he would like to spend some time with her. He waits for her reply, figuring that she either is in a meeting or has not made it in yet. He closes the instant messenger but stays logged in just in case Tonya replies before lunch.

Around 1:00 p.m., Devon returns from lunch. He is checking the instant messenger when his ringing cell phone interrupts him.

"Devon here."

"Hello, Devon! This is Samantha."

"Hi, Samantha. What's up?"

"I just called because I wanted to see if you wanted to go to the movies or out somewhere tonight?"

"That sounds good, but I am not sure right now because my brother is supposed to be coming into town tonight or tomorrow."

"I understand. Just let me know if you want to get together."

"I'll call you later, okay?"

He hangs up the phone and remembers that he needs to call Vanessa.

"Hello, Vanessa Lewis speaking."

"Hi, Ms. Lewis. This is Mr. McNeil. How are you today?"

"I am doing great! And yourself?"

"Things couldn't be better over here. Hey! Vanessa, do you want to do something fun, exciting, and a little dangerous?"

"Sure, as long as I won't kill myself."

"Of course not. Tonight is old school night at the Crystal Palace."

"I've heard about that place. Devon, I haven't been on roller skates in years."

"Don't worry. I roller skate all the time. I will catch you if you fall. Come on! Do something different for a change."

"What the hell! Okay, I'll go, Devon!"

"Ah, man! I forgot my brother is coming into town this weekend. I am not sure if he is coming tonight or tomorrow. I'll check with my mom to see when he is coming."

"I understand, Devon. When you find out, just let me know, and I am sure we can do something this week."

Devon hangs up the phone. He tries to decide with whom and where he will go this evening. He has three dates for the weekend, and he wants to make the best of it. So, he evaluates each opportunity. *Let me see*, he ponders…*First there is Tonya. I was with her last night. I don't know about seeing her two nights in a row. Then there is Samantha. I haven't been with her in a while; I might need to take her up on her offer. Besides, she knows exactly what I like. Oh! I can't forget about Vanessa and those hips. Man! I don't know. I tell you what. I guess I*

168

will hook up with Samantha tonight, because I know what's on her mind. Then on Saturday, I will take out Vanessa. I still need to work on her.

As for Tonya, I've already informed her that my brother will be in town this weekend, so she will know that if she does not hear from me, I must be spending time with my family. This way I don't have to worry about her bugging me all weekend. On Sunday, I will spend some quality time with her. Yeah! That's what I'll do. He leans back in his chair, picks up the phone and calls Samantha.

"Hello, Samantha. This is Devon. I am calling to take you up on your offer for a movie and whatever else tonight."

"Great! Trust me when I say you won't regret it."

Devon shuts down his computer for the day and heads home to get ready for his busy weekend, starting with Samantha. While getting dressed, he calls Tonya and Vanessa to let them know that he will be at his mother's spending time with his family, but he will call them over the weekend.

Before he walks out the door, Devon looks around to make sure he has everything. He has his wallet, car keys, and gym bag. Every Saturday morning he goes to the gym to play a few pick-up games of basketball.

Later that evening, after the movie, Devon and Samantha return to her place for a little rest and relaxation. Actually, it is more like sex and relaxation. The next morning, Devon leaves Samantha's and heads to the gym. Knowing that Tonya is aware that he plays ball every Saturday morning, he calls Tonya when he arrives at the gym. That way she will hear balls bouncing in the background. Once he feels like he has spent enough time on the phone with Tonya in order to convince her that she still is a top priority, he ends the call and begins to play a game of basketball.

While he is on the court, he hears his cell phone ring. He asks one of the guys on the sideline to check the caller ID for him. Larry, who does the honors, yells out, "It's Vanessa, dog!" Devon signals okay with a nod.

After he has played four or five games, he calls back Vanessa.

"Hello, Vanessa!"

"Hi, Devon. Sounds like you're at the gym."

"Yes, I am."

"You could have called me after you left."

"I know, but I haven't spoken to you in the last few hours, and it sure sounds good to hear your sweet voice over the phone. I would rather hear it in person. My brother is supposed to hang out with some of his old friends, so if you want to hook up later, we can."

"I would love to."

"I should be finished playing in a couple of hours. So do you want to get together about six or seven?"

"That's fine!"

"I'll call you when I'm on my way."

Devon plays one more game and then heads to the locker room to shower and dress. While he is in the shower, he hears his cell phone ringing again. When he gets out of the shower, he looks at the caller ID. It is his mom's number, so he calls her back. When she answers, he hears his brother's voice in the background. His mom tells him that Tim has just made it in. Devon hangs up the phone, dresses, and heads to his mother's house.

Devon sees Tim standing outside talking to a neighbor. He honks the horn, and Tim turns around. He is obviously impressed by the black convertible Devon is driving, because he immediately approaches the car, grinning from ear to ear. Devon asks Tim if he wants to hit the streets that night with him in his Mercedes Benz 500 SL.

"Devon, I don't know," Tim says.

"You never like to hang out with me anymore. Why is that?"

"Devon, you know, lil' brother, I love you. It's just we are at two different points in our lives. You still like to hang out and chase women. I am past that point in my life. I'm looking to settle down and start a family."

"Oh, here we go again. Mom already preached that sermon to me many times while you were gone."

"I see it hasn't worked."

"Tim, just hang out with your brother and catch up on old times. What do you say?"

"Okay, but don't be taking me to one of those strip clubs. You know I don't like those places."

"Okay. I won't."

Devon suggests they hang out at his place and leave from there to hit the streets. After a beer or two and a game of dominos, he realizes that he has not called Vanessa back. He picks up the phone and dials her number. She answers the phone.

"Hello."

"Hello, Vanessa. I am sorry that I am just getting back with you. I have a bit of bad news."

"What is it? Are you hurt?"

"No! I've been so occupied with my brother, Tim, I forgot to call you. He wants to hang out with me instead of his old friends tonight. He has been away overseas for a while, so I thought I would take him to a couple of the new hot spots. I know we had plans, and I would still like to see you tonight, but I do need to spend some time with Tim."

"Go ahead and hang out with your brother, and we can get together another time."

"Thanks, Vanessa. Hey! I was thinking about taking him over to the new Platinum Club later on tonight. You are more than welcome to meet us out there."

"You know I don't like going to clubs. I'll see, but I can't promise anything."

"Okay! I'll save a dance for you if you decide to come out."

Devon and Tim dress and are en route to the Platinum Club when Devon remembers that he has not called Tonya back. He brushes it off and decides that he will call in the morning.

Inside the club, Devon is on his third round of drinks, standing at the bar talking. Tim is starting to feel uncomfortable about the environment in light of where he is at in his life and relationship with God, but he is with his brother and family is family.

"Tim, look! Do you see that woman wearing the blue top?"

"What about her?"

"You don't like that? She is sexy, sexy."

"She's all right. I know her from back in the day. Her name is Crystal. She's a player just like you. That is why I had to sit her down."

"I hear that. Let her know if she is ready to move into the starting line up, she can give me a call. I can handle her."

Crystal walks over to Tim and says hello. Tim then introduces her to Devon.

"What's up, Crystal? I want you to meet my brother, Devon."

"Hi, Devon."

"Hel…lo, Crystal," Devon replies.

"Tim, it is a pleasant surprise to see you. I haven't seen you in a while…How have you been?"

"Cool. Very busy. You know, handling my business."

"You should call me some time so we can stay in touch."

Tim smiles and says, "Okay," but inside he is thinking, *You have lost your damn mind.*

Crystal turns and begins to walk away. Tim, Devon and

every man with eyes cannot help but take another long look at that body as she leaves. After seeing her booty, Devon turns to the bartender and says, "Bartender, another round of drinks. This time, more Remy than orange juice."

After the bartender makes Devon's drinks, he encourages Tim to walk around so they can check out the ladies. As they walk near the dance floor, Devon feels a pinch on his butt. He turns to see who the culprit is. It is Samantha. With a mischievous grin on her face, she grabs Devon by his arm and pulls him close to her. He thinks to himself, *I remember seeing her with an attractive girlfriend at the grocery store the other day. I wonder if she came with her tonight?* This is valuable information for him, because it will help him decide which woman he decides to call for a nightcap. Devon would spend another night with Samantha if he could help his brother hook up with her friend. Even though Tim has been preaching to Devon about being a one woman's man, he feels Tim is overdue for some fun. He introduces Samantha to his brother and asks her if she came out alone. She tells him that her friend Kathy is at the bar getting drinks.

Samantha motions to Kathy to hurry and come back.

"What's up, girl?"

"You remember Devon, and this is his brother, Tim. Guys, this is Kathy."

"Hello, Kathy. It's nice to meet you," Tim replies.

"Likewise."

"Okay, while you two are standing there eyeing each

other, Devon, do you want to dance?"

Devon and Samantha hit the dance floor. The DJ plays one of the hottest songs of the year, a song you can definitely get your freak on, and that is exactly what Samantha does. She works it, freaks it, and grinds it. Not to be outdone, Devon turns and gets a little freaky himself. Then he looks into the crowd and sees Vanessa walking toward the bar. He quickly straightens up and immediately excuses himself when the song is over. He thanks Samantha for the dance and explains that he is going to the men's room. He escorts Samantha off the dance floor and heads toward the men's room, but not before making a slight detour around the bar. He walks up behind Vanessa just as the bartender takes her drink order.

"The lady will have a Cosmopolitan with a twist of lime."

As Vanessa turns to see the mystery man, she realizes it is Devon.

"Hello, Mr. McNeil. I decided to take you up on the offer and hang for a minute, but not too late."

Devon spots an empty table and asks Vanessa if she wants to sit and talk. He picks up her drink and heads toward the empty table, conveniently located in a corner of the club.

After three or four songs, Tim and Kathy make their way off the dance floor and walk toward the bar. Kathy does not see Samantha anywhere. She asks Tim to walk around with her to see if they can find Samantha and Devon. Tim leads the way and notices Devon sitting at a table with another sexy woman. He quickly turns from their direction, trying to prevent Kathy from seeing Devon. It is too late.

"I don't see them over here," Tim says.

"That looks like Devon in the corner. Actually, that is him sitting over there," Kathy remarks.

"Where? That sure is him." Tim pretends to strain his eyes.

Kathy wants to see who is seated with Devon, so she asks Tim to walk over to the table with her.

"Devon, have you seen Samantha?" she asks.

"No, I haven't seen her since we left the dance floor," Devon answers.

Tim leans over and whispers something in Devon's ear. Devon then introduces Tim, Vanessa, and Kathy to one another. He introduces Tim as his brother and Kathy as a friend of a friend.

"Would you like to join us?" Vanessa asks.

Tim declines before Kathy can answer. He does not want to interfere with Devon's game. Kathy can't wait to tell Samantha and makes an excuse to leave the scene. As she walks around the club, she finally runs into Samantha and tells her that Devon is seated in another room with some woman named Vanessa.

Samantha shakes her head and says, "That's Devon. That's why we are not together now. Once a player, always a player."

Back at the table, Devon and Vanessa have an intense conversation about possibly hooking up later. A group of women walks by the table. One of the women bumps into Devon's chair and gives Vanessa a long stare. Vanessa notices that the woman keeps staring at her.

"Damn," Vanessa exclaims.

"What's wrong, Vanessa?" Devon asks.

"The woman standing at the end of the bar keeps staring at me and giving me these dirty looks. I have no idea who she is."

Devon turns around, curious to see the woman who is staring. "Yeah, I see what you mean. She looks familiar. Aw! I know who she is. That's Tonya. We have gone out a couple times, but nothing serious," Devon says nonchalantly.

Vanessa looks at Devon and gives him a small grin.

"It's getting late, and I am getting ready to go, Devon. Will you walk me to my car? Maybe you can stop by after you drop Tim off."

"Sure. Let me find Tim."

Devon's moment of truth is upon him. The woman he has been wanting is now ready to take their friendship to the next level, and Devon is not about to mess up this opportunity.

Devon, feeling a little stress from Tonya but nothing he feels he can't handle, bumps into Tim as he leaves the dance floor. "Hey, Devon, where is Vanessa?"

"She is waiting for me in the other room, and I am going to her house tonight, but first I have to take care of something."

"What are you talking about, man?"

"You don't know Tonya, but she's here, and she walked by when I was sitting with Vanessa. Say, dog, walk over here with

"I'll tell you this. Pray that you don't have a daughter someday and that she doesn't end up dating someone like you. That would be more justice than you could handle."

me. We are going to act like we are making our rounds through the club and stop over at Tonya's table."

"See, Devon, that's what I am talking about. You've always come to me looking for help to get you out of trouble with these women. I told you before, I'm past playing games. I'm on a different level now. Respect that."

"You're my brother. Don't let me down."

"I'll tell you this. Pray that you don't have a daughter someday and that she doesn't end up dating someone like you. That would be more justice than you could handle."

Devon and Tim head over to the table where Tonya is seated with a couple of her girlfriends. Tonya gets up and goes to the bar when she notices the two of them heading her way. She doesn't want to have to explain anything to her girls about Devon being with another woman. They meet at the bar.

"Hello, Devon."

"What's up, Tonya?"

"I'm surprised to see you here. I thought you were going to be over at your mother's house spending time with your family."

"I was, but my brother wanted to get out and mingle a little bit."

"I see he is not the only one mingling tonight."

Before she can finish her thought, Devon says, "Tonya, this is my brother Tim. Tim, this is Tonya, the young lady I have been writing and telling you about."

"Nice to meet you, Tim,"

"Nice to meet you, too, Tonya," Tim replies. Tim can feel the tension brewing from Tonya and doesn't want to have any part of it. "Devon, I see Kathy over there, so I am going to go get my groove on, and I will holla at you two in a few."

"So are you enjoying yourself? It looks like you are. Devon, who was that woman you were sitting with earlier?"

"That's Vanessa. It was funny bumping into her tonight. She heads the accounting department for Chambers Studio."

"Is she the person you have been meeting with for Chambers Studios? You don't have to answer that. I can figure it out."

At this point, Devon is weighing his options. There are a couple of ways he can handle the situation. He thinks about the decision he needs to make right then. *I can leave with Tonya and spend the rest of the night with her, showing her that Vanessa isn't anybody special to me, or I can take Vanessa up on her offer and take the chance of Tonya not wanting to see*

I CAN LEAVE WITH TONYA AND SPEND THE REST OF THE NIGHT WITH HER, SHOWING HER THAT VANESSA ISN'T ANYBODY SPECIAL TO ME, OR I CAN TAKE VANESSA UP ON HER OFFER AND TAKE THE CHANCE OF TONYA NOT WANTING TO SEE ME AGAIN. BUT I'M CONFIDENT THAT TONYA WILL GET OVER IT IN A FEW DAYS AND BE BACK. AND, AFTER ONE MORE WEEK, EVEN IF TONYA DECIDES TO LEAVE ME, I FIGURE I CAN MOVE VANESSA INTO TONYA'S SPOT WITHOUT SKIPPING A BEAT.

me again. But I'm confident that Tonya will get over it in a few days and be back. And, after one more week, even if Tonya decides to leave me, I figure I can move Vanessa into Tonya's spot without skipping a beat.

So what does he do? He rolls the dice and sees what will

happen next.

"Tonya, you know I care about you. Who do I spend all my time with? I enjoy the time we spend together, but we have never sat down and talked about 'us' together. Tonya, this is not the place to start a discussion of this magnitude. I suggest we talk about this later."

"Later! When, Devon?"

"Later on tonight, or in the morning, but later, Tonya! I need to find Tim, because he was talking about leaving."

"Just answer one thing for me, Devon. Does this mean we can see other people?"

"Tonya, we have always been able to see other people. We never communicated to each other that we were seeing each other exclusively. So, yes, if you see someone you like and want to talk to him, there is nothing I can say about it. Now excuse me, please. I need to find Tim."

Tonya stands there with a hateful look on her face and one tear hanging on at the corner of her eye as Devon turns and walks away without saying another word.

Tonya pats her eyes dry and returns to the table where her girlfriends are sitting. She does not want to seem upset, so she grabs her purse and tells her friends that she is leaving because she is getting a headache.

Devon finds Tim and asks him to meet him outside. He proceeds to the valet's station to pick up Vanessa's car. As he waits for the valet to return with Vanessa's car, he sees Tonya race out of the parking lot.

Devon contemplates whether he should call Tonya before he heads to Vanessa's place. But he knows that if he calls, he could possibly lose control, so he decides to wait for Tonya to call him instead.

In Devon's car, before dropping Tim off at his house, Tim has a few things he wants to get off his chest.

"Devon, you make it bad for the rest of us guys who are trying to do right by women."

"THAT'S WHAT MAKES ME SO MAD, BECAUSE IT'S MEN LIKE YOU AND DAD THAT MAKE IT HARD FOR US GOOD MEN LIKE MYSELF. WOMEN THEN TURN AROUND AND THINK THAT ALL MEN ARE NO GOOD BECAUSE OF MEN LIKE YOU TWO."

"Oh brother. Here we go again."

"You're going to listen. I am disappointed in you, Devon. Do you know that what you are doing doesn't make you more of a man?"

"Oh well."

"That's what makes me so mad, because it's men like you and Dad that make it hard for us *good* men like myself. Women then turn around and think that all men are no good because of men like you two, but I still love you."

It becomes obvious that Tim's speech isn't having any effect on Devon.

"Devon, do you hear me talking to you? It's no use, but you'll see one day."

After dropping Tim off, he heads over to Vanessa's place. Not too long after Devon walks through the door, they are wrapped up in the satin sheets on Vanessa's king-size canopy bed.

Over the next few days, he is preparing to move Vanessa into Tonya's place. They speak more frequently and trade email messages. They also begin to spend time together, just as Devon and Tonya had spent time together. While he is on the phone with Vanessa, Devon receives another incoming call. He asks Vanessa to hold and answers the call.

"Devon Mc Neil speaking."

"Hello, Devon."

"Tonya! How are you doing? I am glad you called me. I have been missing you these last few days. I was hoping you would call me. I wanted to let things cool down before I called you. I was hoping we could still see one another."

"I don't know, Devon. I was calling just to check on you and see how you are doing."

"Tonya, can we talk about this in person? Tonight?"

"Devon, I don't know."

"We need to have this conversation in person, not over the

phone. Can I meet you at your house at 6:30 p.m.? Please? You know you are my BOO!"

"All right, Devon. You can come over. See you then."

He returns to the line where Vanessa is holding.

"I'm sorry, Boo, but that was a business call I had to take."

He leans back in his chair with his hands crossed behind his head thinking about how he has manipulated the game in a strategic manner: moving the pieces in the right place at the right time and not afraid of taking risks when dealing with women's hearts in order to maintain his casual sex partners.

I could continue with this scenario, but until the Tonyas of the world learn the lesson that a man does not make or define a woman and take more control over the way the dating game is played, there will always be conceited men like Devon who feel every woman needs a man like them.

As in the game of chess, Tonya yells, "CHECK" and Devon, well, what can he say but "CHECKMATE!" …Game Over….

11

CHAPTER ELEVEN
WHAT WOMEN MUST DO

L adies, first you have to realize that most men view relationships with women like a game where there are winners and losers. Of course, men are very competitive and play to win at any cost. Men know that women are emotional creatures and that they will let their feelings overrule their better judgment at times. A woman who is emotionally invested in a man will do anything and everything to please him. If a man can get a woman to make decisions based on how she feels about him instead of what is in her best interest, then he wins. Checkmate! Take the different case studies that were described earlier. Once these women realized they were not in a committed relationship, their better judgment would have been to keep away from these men. But their hearts and the hope that these men would change and be with them

YOU FIND YOURSELF LYING ACROSS THE BED CLUTCHING A PILLOW WITH TEARS RUNNING DOWN YOUR FACE AND YOUR MIND REPLAYING ALL THE EVENTS THAT HAVE LED UP TO THIS MOMENT.

only brought them back again and again.

You know in your mind that some relationships with some men are just mistakes. But often the heart holds on to the sweet things they did, the way they made you feel, and the passionate love you shared while in the bedroom. (And I use the word "love" very loosely.) But, along the way, you have to compare what he is saying to what he is doing and question whether his actions and words agree. If you allow either a man's actions or his words to overrule each other, then you will find yourself feeling used and betrayed, in other words, CHECKMATED.

After being Checkmated, there will come a point where you feel like you are at the end of your rope and don't know how you got yourself into the mess that you are in. You are looking in the mirror with teary, red eyes, looking at the broken reflection of yourself, and questioning where it all went wrong. You find yourself lying across the bed clutching a pillow with tears running down your face and your mind replaying all the events that have led up to this moment.

When these things happen, here is what you must do...

First of all, stop doubting yourself and questioning the things you could have done better. Just realize that if you cook for the player, clean for the player—even if you give him the world—there is no guarantee that you will satisfy him. It doesn't matter who you are. It doesn't matter what you can do. It just doesn't matter. A man is going to do what he wants to do, when he wants to do it. He makes a conscious decision when he meets you as to the category he is going to put you in. He normally decides very early in the game if you are a potential wife or someone he wants around for sex. If you are placed in the wife's pool, you will be treated with more respect. He soon will begin to share more of his things freely and look for ways to make your life easier. In the booty call classification, you get treated with respect to a limited degree. He will only do the bare minimum to keep you around and content with the relationship. It doesn't matter what you do for or to him. He is going to continue to be the selfish person he is and try to romance as many women as he can into a casual sexual relationship without commitments. The question is...will you allow this?

Next, you have to come to the realization that you are feeling this way not because of anything that you could have or should have done better. What has happened is a result of a choice that he made and not because you have possibly not done your part. At some point, at least in his mind, it became all about him…and it had nothing to do with you. What you are dealing with is a result of something far beyond your control.

Once you realize that there is nothing you can do to change the way he feels about you, then you have to let go. Let go of the guilt. Let go of the disappointment. Let go of the fear. You have to get yourself together so that you are ready to love again and are not taking the baggage from the broken relationship into what might be a new and healthier situation. You must

LET GO OF THE GUILT. LET GO OF THE DISAPPOINTMENT. LET GO OF THE FEAR. YOU HAVE TO GET YOURSELF TOGETHER SO THAT YOU ARE READY TO LOVE AGAIN AND ARE NOT TAKING THE BAGGAGE FROM THE BROKEN RELATIONSHIP INTO WHAT MIGHT BE A NEW AND HEALTHIER SITUATION.

know that there is indeed the possibility that you may win the game and have the committed relationship that you deserve and desire. And you must be open and ready for the person to come into your life who may not at all be interested in the game. Because while the majority of men are players, not all men are players.

And finally, after you have experienced weeks of sleepless nights, tossing and turning, trying to find peace in the darkness of your mind, you may be awakened by a familiar voice that you may

> BECAUSE WHILE THE MAJORITY OF MEN ARE PLAYERS, NOT ALL MEN ARE PLAYERS.

think is that of the man you love lying next to you…, but it isn't. If you listen closely, you will find that the soft but strong masculine voice is still a familiar one. It is one that has called out to you before and one that you may have been ignoring over the years. The voice will say to you in a whisper, "I can restore your peace, and I can mend your broken heart. The only thing I ask of you is to put your trust in Me." The voice is that of the only person who can solve all your problems. It belongs to the Lord Jesus Christ. He will sympathetically call you to

> THE VOICE WILL SAY TO YOU IN A WHISPER, "I CAN RESTORE YOUR PEACE, AND I CAN MEND YOUR BROKEN HEART. THE ONLY THING I ASK OF YOU IS TO PUT YOUR TRUST IN ME."

your knees, and He will soon give you the clarity of thought you need to get past the pain. He will help you to realize that He has always been there, calling out to you, and that He is using this event, and many of your other past heartaches, to bring you closer to Him.

How do I know this to be true?

If you would have told me that on my wedding day that my bride-to-be would leave me standing alone at the altar, I would have laughed in disbelief. I never thought that a woman could be capable of such a thing! I always thought that it would be the man, if anyone, who would leave at such a time. And, I also felt that all women wanted and needed a man like me. A successful, attractive—and willing—man. But I soon found out that I was wrong.

I am living proof that these things do not just happen to women and that I was not the man I thought I was.

I, too, have laid across my bed with tears running down my face, clutching my pillow, and my mind playing every event over and over again. I, too, have looked in the mirror asking myself what I could have done differently. There were many nights when I would cry myself to sleep, hoping that sleep would take me to a tranquil place were my heartache could not follow me. I longed for just one peaceful night of sleep. But even on the nights I was able to sleep, I realized that only my body would benefit…and only to a small degree. My mind never seemed to rest.

Even in my sleep, my mind would relive that dreadful day

over and over again. For weeks I would wake up in the middle of the night, tossing and turning from my dreams and crying out to her, hoping that she would somehow change her mind.

But then I would hear the whisper. Yes, that familiar whisper. Every time I would hear this voice, I would rise up out of bed, look out across the room searching for the person whose voice I had heard.

I remember hearing my biological father often preach that it is with the mind and heart that we serve the Lord Jesus Christ and that our God is a jealous one. With this, I questioned how could I hear and serve Him and have my mind so clouded with fantasies, hopes, and dreams of her. She became my obsession! It wasn't until the night I finally recognized that it was the Lord's voice I was hearing and that He was calling out to me that I climbed out of bed, got down on my knees, and then I asked the Lord for the strength to take back the power that I had given her. I understood then that the building of my new life…a new me…started with my mind, my heart and relationship with God.

The mind is the chessboard where the game is played. Within my mind there was a constant struggle between my emotions and my logical thinking. My logical thinking was building me up and telling me that there was still hope for a new meaningful relationship. It was reminding me that I could get up and that I was not worthless. But my emotions were tearing me down and telling me that I was defeated. I could hear them tell me that I couldn't get up and that nobody wanted me. The fight I had to win was in my mind. With my mind now more focused on the Lord and what He was whispering to me, I was able to overcome this struggle. Through the power and grace of God, I took back control of my mind and my emotions. With my self-esteem now in place, I was able to get back on track and to get myself back together. You can, too.

I AM NOW ABLE TO CLOSE OUT THAT OLD CHAPTER IN MY LIFE AND START WRITING THE NEW ONE!

I AM NOW ABLE TO CLOSE OUT THAT OLD CHAPTER IN MY LIFE AND START WRITING THE NEW ONE!

Having moved past the pain, I now realize a whole new world awaits me. It took a while, but I finally made it through. I know life can hurt. And you can believe that I have been hurt. But I hold no resentment toward the woman who left me, because if it were not for her, I would not be in the place that I am…closer to the Lord and more equipped to love again. Now that I know for sure who I am, and with God operating in my life, I am prepared to say the words "I Do" the next time with the confidence that I can be the friend, father, lover, and husband a woman deserves.

APPENDIX
QUESTIONS A WOMAN SHOULD ASK HERSELF...

1. Are you an independent woman...or a codependent enabler?

Women are now fully embracing their newfound independence. Men, on the other hand, are using this newfound strength to their advantage. Over the years, women have become more independent and men have become more dependent. Most women are no longer waiting around for a man to walk into their lives to be the provider. Most men feel that since women have the same opportunities that they do, then they should not have to bare the load of being the sole provider. As a result, women enter in these codependent relationships that are destined to fail. Lots of women have falsely bought into thinking that they make their own money, they pay their own bills, and that they don't need a man. But they also conclude that it would be nice to have someone around for companionship. What women do not realize is that this way of thinking is a result of the games men play. Because the field is so flooded with game-playing men, it appears to women that there just are not enough quality men around. So women have developed the attitude that they must find their own happiness within themselves.

Men have used the woman's independence to their advantage. Men think that women are judging them based on the amount of money that they make and how well they are able to take care of them. And men have not been quiet about their displeasure with having to always pick up the tab when they are out on a date with a woman. This causes men to label most, if not all, women as money chasers or gold diggers.

Women who are independent want to distinguish themselves from the gold diggers by offering to pick up the tab or, better yet, inviting a man out for the evening. And most women see nothing wrong with doing that. They feel they make enough money, so it is not that big of a deal.

But a man thinks that a woman spending money on him is a big deal. A man figures that women can pay all their bills during the first week of the month, be broke for the rest of the month and still be able to go out and have a good time. Why? In the traditional way of dating there is a presumption that the man will cover the expenses of the outing. The man, on the other hand, has far different plans for the money he has after paying bills. He figures that whatever he has left over now has to be budgeted and used for his entertainment for the rest of the month. He knows that if the woman pays for some of the outings, then that will free up more of his money to spend on other women. Every man has a dating budget. And if you want to know where you stand with him, look at how much of his discretionary budget is he spending on you per month. If you are not getting 90 to 95 percent, rest assured that some other woman, or women, is getting the percentage that you are not.

If you allow men to be cheap, then they will always be cheap. However, if he knows that you will accept nothing but the best, then he will put his best foot forward. This is not to say that being a "gold digger" is the way to go. But if you sell yourself short, then he will continue to treat you that way.

THE GAMES MEN PLAY

THE BOTTOM LINE IS, IF YOU KEEP ENDING UP WITH THE SAME TYPE OF MEN AND IN THE SAME TYPE OF NEGATIVE SITUATIONS, THEN THERE IS SOMETHING IN YOU THAT THEY SEE THAT YOU NEED TO SEE AND CHANGE.

Don't be content with being a $5 million actress, when you are instead a $20 million super star.

The bottom line is, if you keep ending up with the same type of men and in the same type of negative situations, then there is something in you that they see that you need to see and change.

2. **Will he be your life jacket...or drive you to a straight jacket?**

A woman has to determine if a man will add to the quality of her life, or will he drain the very life she has out of her. She will have to evaluate whether he is giving her what she deserves and is worth, or will he make her question her very value? Does he encourage you and support you? Can you see him as your "backbone?" Or, will he break your spirit and be such a burden that he will cause your spine to curve? In the midst of trouble, will he be there to save your life, or will he

DOES YOUR RELATIONSHIP WITH YOUR MAN CAUSE FOR YOUR RELATIONSHIP WITH GOD TO INCREASE OR DETERIORATE?

just make your life crazy? Will he be your spiritual covering, or is his mind just on having you under the covers? And especially, does your relationship with your man cause for your relationship with God to increase or deteriorate?

3. Are you a prime time sitcom...or a late-night rerun?

The major television networks air their most popular television shows and the ones that bring in the highest ratings between the hours of 8:00 p.m. and 10:00 p.m., EST. Both large and small companies pay top dollar to those television networks to have their commercials shown during those times. It would be a financial disaster for a television network to air a program that wasn't popular with their viewing audience during the time when they have the most viewers. Their ratings would go down, and the companies would stop paying top dollar. The companies would rather spend their dollars where they will get the best return on their investment.

Men view women in this same way. They either see the woman as good enough to be seen in public, during the hours where they may be seen the most, or they see her as someone whose value is limited only to the late-night hours. And please know that the decision to place the women in one category or

THEY EITHER SEE THE WOMAN AS GOOD ENOUGH TO BE SEEN IN PUBLIC, DURING THE HOURS WHERE THEY MAY BE SEEN THE MOST, OR THEY SEE HER AS SOMEONE WHOSE VALUE IS LIMITED ONLY TO THE LATE-NIGHT HOURS.

another has nothing to do with her beauty. What matters is what a man perceives that a woman may bring to the table. It is based on his evaluation of her ability to offer him what he is looking for, and only he will know what it takes to move out of the late- night T.V. rotation and into the prime time viewing hours. Be it cooking, cleaning, great sex or a good time, what he is looking for varies from man to man and from situation to situation. But regardless of what a man decides and why, what a woman must know is that if he's not spending time with her between 8 and 10, then she is out of the prime time rotation.

4.   **What is his sign? HIV +...or −**

In recent years, there has been a lot of discussion about the cost of sexual promiscuity and issues such as "down low" bi-sexuality, homosexuality and AIDS. Now, more than ever, women are aware of the physical and emotional dangers of dealing with men in uncommitted relationships. Women read books and magazines and listen to all types of advice on what to do to protect themselves. Yet, with all the wealth of information at their disposal, women often fail to do what it takes to protect themselves from disease and harm.

Women still do not ask the right questions. In today's society, asking certain questions is considered taboo or too personal. However, within the context of dating, a question that could possibly prevent harm, or even save a life, is never too personal. Instead of using all your effort searching for clues to his hidden sexual preferences and spending your time guessing as

WITHIN THE CONTEXT OF DATING, A QUESTION THAT COULD POSSIBLY PREVENT HARM, OR EVEN SAVE A LIFE, IS NEVER TOO PERSONAL.

to who else he may be sleeping with, just ask the question. Ask him out right and gauge his answers carefully. If he hesitates or becomes offended, then he is not the safest man to be with.

5. Is your relationship leading to the altar, or do you need to alter... the relationship?

The idea that a man is not capable or never wants to commit is untrue. All men not only have the ability to commit, they almost all want to commit at some time. But the problem comes in because the time frame in which a man is ready to commit is often not in sync with the time frame of the woman.

A man's time of commitment is often directly related to his success in his career. As long as a man sees himself as

INSTEAD OF USING ALL YOUR EFFORT SEARCHING FOR CLUES TO HIS HIDDEN SEXUAL PREFERENCES AND SPENDING YOUR TIME GUESSING AS TO WHO ELSE HE MAY BE SLEEPING WITH, JUST ASK THE QUESTION. ASK HIM OUTRIGHT AND GAUGE HIS ANSWERS CAREFULLY.

climbing the corporate or career ladder and capable of reaching a higher level of financial stability, he will continue his quest for what he considers a "higher quality" of woman. As he moves to a higher income bracket, he also moves into what he considers a larger and possible better pool of women.

Once a man feels that his income level has reached its plateau, he stops to evaluate the pool of women now available to him. It is then that he begins to seriously consider the best candidates in that pool. The question is not if he will find a woman but when, because he will indeed go after what he considers to be the best of the pool. Once he selects the best candidate, he then often proceeds to establish or cultivate a healthier relationship to the degree that he believes it will lead to a long and prosperous life together.

So the question for women becomes a two-part question. First, you must determine if it is the man's time. Has he reached is career plateau or some other type of plateau and therefore is he ready to seek commitment? But you also have to consider your placement in the pool…or if you are in the pool at all. You have to ask yourself if the man has moved himself beyond you and whether he perceives to be you his best choice. It is nothing you can do to assure your spot…This all depends on the man's perception of your place. However, you must be aware that many men evaluate you…and your place-

BEFORE YOU DECLARE THAT HE IS THE LOVE OF YOUR LIFE AND YOU WANT TO SPEND A LIFETIME OF LOVING HIM, MAKE SURE THAT THE RESPECT AND LOVE THAT GOD WOULD WANT FOR YOU TO SHOW EACH OTHER IS CONSISTENTLY EVIDENT IN YOUR RELATIONSHIP. OTHERWISE, CHECKMATE.

ment in their life...based on their ability to move between the pools. Ultimately, Women, don't lower your standards just to get a man. Before you declare that he is the love of your life and you want to spend a lifetime of loving him, make sure that the respect and love that God would want for you to show each other is consistently evident in your relationship. Otherwise, CHECKMATE.

AUTHOR PROFILE

Author Mark Crutcher has a new outlook on life. Within the span of two years, he has written a national bestselling tell-all book.

In his first published book entitled *Checkmate: The Games Men Play,* Mr. Crutcher writes an empowering book for women to gain an understanding of the dating process and tricks and techniques used by players to win women's hearts, souls, minds, and of course, their bodies. A former player, pimp and even a gigolo, Mr. Crutcher has given up his players' card in an effort to help relinquish the heavy burden on his heart. *Checkmate* provides uncut and uncensored access into the secrets that men vow never to reveal.

Professionally, Mr. Crutcher has been a corporate executive in the field of human resources for Fortune 500 companies, directing their recruiting efforts for the past eight years before pursuing his writing career full time. Born in Memphis, TN and currently residing in Desoto, TX, he is the parent of two loving children. Mr. Crutcher is also a playwright and movie screenplay writer.